Freeing Nicole

A twisty whodunit

D.J. Maughan

Hulyeseg Inc

Dedication

For you, Hocky-Nocky-Fruity-Fru. Twenty-seven years ago, I stood by your bedside saying goodbye, knowing I'd never see you again in this life. I wonder where you'd be now if you hadn't had the physical challenges. What you'd be doing. How my life would have been blessed to have you still in it. I love you and count myself lucky to have you as my sister. I miss you.

Foreword

Stay tuned at the end of the novel for a special note about the real Nicole. Also, access a free short story about Hank and Joyce's first day working together.

Chapter 1
Sherry

The thin man with a pale mask concealing half his face flips his black cape as he turns away from the girl dressed in a white gown and stares at the enormous challenger who has just entered the stage. The theater lights glare to reveal the challenger holding a sword in front of himself. They're in the Phantom's lair, and I marvel at the craftsmanship of the stage props. Who built this? Someone who has talent.

"Stay away from her," the gigantic challenger commands.

"No, Raul," the girl pleads, extending her hand toward him.

"It's okay, Nicole," he says, then hits his palm to his forehead and shakes his head, looking at the director backstage.

The man in the mask and the woman join him in looking to the director for guidance. After several seconds, all cast members regain their composure.

"Sorry, I mean Christine," the challenger says.

My mother, seated beside me, looks over and smiles. Her eyes return to the stage where she lovingly watches her only granddaughter, Nicole, play the part of Christine in the performance she's talked about incessantly for months. My eyes linger on my mother. Her decline is becoming more pronounced, and I find myself watching her every day with increasing anxiety. Her hair is as white as snow. Wrinkles cover her skin. Her breathing is labored, and her shoulders stoop. She'll turn eighty-six this year, and I know she won't see eighty-seven.

It's been three years since Daddy died. A fact she reminds me of every day. Six months since I lost Ron. How can I bear it? How can I lose another person I love? Only Nicole will be left.

A panic rises in my chest, and I push it down, forcing my attention back to the stage and my daughter. She and the other kids in the high school special education class have been working on this play every day for two months. It's all Nicole has talked about. She loves being the center of attention, and the opportunity to play Christine in *The Phantom of the Opera* is almost more than she can fathom. Tonight is her time to shine, even if it's December but not a Christmas play.

The challenger turns back to the Phantom and extends his sword, point first. The lighting dims, and the effect, along with the exceptional set design, sends a chill down my spine.

"So be it," the Phantom says, skulking to the other end of the stage and withdrawing a sword from a scabbard. He raises and lowers the sword, feeling the weight in his hand as he walks back to the middle of the stage and holds the point toward Raul, the challenger. "Let it be war upon you," he says, stepping forward.

The two boys clink swords and circle each other. Raul swings his sword first and the Phantom sidesteps. One of his shoes is untied, and he trips over it, falling to the ground and dropping the sword.

A couple of boys in the audience, just a row in front of us, snicker and clamp their hands over their mouths. Their mother turns and glares, shushing them. Their shoulders bump up and down with laughter.

Raul steps forward, towering over the Phantom in a menacing pose, but rather than attack, he drops his sword to his side and extends his hand.

The Phantom looks up at him, then offers his hand, and Raul pulls him to his feet.

"Roy, are you okay?" Raul asks.

The Phantom nods, and Raul pats his shoulder. The Phantom directs him back into position, and the fighting resumes.

"Christine is mine," the Phantom says, returning to character. He lunges at Raul, sword extended. Raul easily meets the challenge, and the blow glances to the side.

The two boys circle each other once again before Raul attacks. He jabs his sword at the Phantom and plunges it into his chest. The Phantom gasps, and his eyes widen in shock. He stumbles backward and falls to the ground. A hush falls over the auditorium as the audience watches in stunned silence, surprised at the departure from the usual script.

From behind the curtain, Georgette Thomas, the high school special education teacher and play director, runs onto the stage. She kneels beside the Phantom, her concern prominent.

"Roy?" she calls, reaching out a hand. "Roy, are you okay?"

She digs at his clothes, ripping away his shirt, exposing his torso.

I gasp along with everyone else in the audience.

Blood covers his chest and grows in an expanding pool beneath him. His body lies lifeless on the stage. Ms. Thomas removes his mask and speaks to him, calling his name. His eyes are wide, his face ashen.

She turns away from him, her face panicked. "We need help. Call 9-1-1!" she shouts.

Chapter 2
Hank

Weary of standing, I pull the chair away from the wall and sit, watching my partner, Detective Joyce Powers, as she examines the body and crime scene. Two uniformed police officers stand beside the coroner, waiting for our examination to be complete. Mine ended several minutes ago. Since then, I've stood watching Joyce, trying to see what she sees—eventually giving in to my desire to sit.

The coroner, a wiry man with a blonde mustache and receding hairline, walks over to me. In a hushed voice, he asks, "Are you about done?"

I look at him, then look back at Joyce, and shrug.

He checks his watch. "I don't want to be out all night."

My thoughts exactly, but I'm not about to let him know that. I don't reply and go on watching Joyce as she drops to her knees and examines the body more closely. After several more minutes, she straightens and puts on a pair of gloves. She picks up the murder weapon and frowns, turning it over in her hands.

"Detective?" the coroner says, stepping closer to her. "Are you done with the body? We'd like to get it out of here."

Joyce looks at him, then at me. I shrug and she nods. "Go ahead."

Another man joins him, and they roll a stretcher with a body bag onto the stage while Joyce walks over to me, holding the sword. I stand to greet her, towering over her.

"I spoke to one officer," I say, motioning to a man in uniform standing by the door. "He said the boy was stabbed by a classmate during a play."

She nods, her eyes never leaving the sword as she scrutinizes it.

"I'm not sure of the name of the play," I say, looking down at my notepad.

"*The Phantom of the Opera*," Joyce says, looking up at me.

I'm not surprised she knows the name. At this point, I could never be surprised by anything she said or did. We've been partners for over a year, and her knowledge of weird, random things never ceases to amaze me. She knows things before they happen. What strikes me as odd is the choice to do this play rather than something Christmas related. It is December after all.

"How many people?"

"In the play?" I ask.

"In the building."

"Maybe fifty or sixty in the audience. Probably another ten or fifteen on the stage or behind it. No idea how many in the rest of the building."

She nods. "Where are they now?"

I shake my head and motion to Officer Mendez. He sees me and comes over.

"Where are all the people who were here when it happened?" I ask.

"In the library."

"All of them?" Joyce asks.

"All but the boy who stabbed him. He and his father are in the special education classroom."

Joyce looks at me and I nod.

"Get their information and release them. Let them go home," I say.

"The boy and his father?" Mendez asks.

Joyce sighs and walks away from us, still examining the sword.

I shake my head and slow my speech, speaking in a gentle tone. "No, the rest of the people who are waiting in the library. Gather all their personal information, including their names and contact information. Get a brief statement. Ask them what they saw and where they were when it happened. Get as many officers as you can spare to help. Get it done quickly and efficiently, then let them go home."

Mendez nods, glances over to Joyce, then walks away.

When he's several feet away, she comes back to me. "Time to go talk to this boy and his father."

Chapter 3
Hank

As we walk down the hallway to the special education classroom, we see Officer Levy standing outside the closed door, waiting for us. She speaks as we approach.

"Detectives."

"How are things, Carol?" Joyce asks.

Carol Levy is a uniformed police officer in the department and has been for about ten years. She's never said it, but I sense animosity when she looks at me. I was hired as Joyce's partner with little experience, and she likely felt passed over. She focuses on Joyce and shakes her head. She puts her hands on her hips, above her belt, and bumps her radio. It comes free and crashes to the floor, sliding along the polished surface to the row of lockers on the far wall.

"Sorry," she says and chases after it. She retrieves the radio and fastens it to her belt as she walks back. Carol looks up at me, then at Joyce. Her cheeks are flushed. "Sorry about that."

Neither of us speaks, waiting for her. She stares at Joyce uncertainly.

Joyce frowns and raises her hands, palms up. "You were saying?"

"Oh, sorry." Carol brings her hands together and rubs her fingers. She looks over her shoulder at the closed door, then steps closer to Joyce, dropping her voice. "That boy in there, the big handicapped one. The one who murdered the other boy. He's being very difficult. We had to restrain him. I wanted you to know what you're stepping into. His father is with him. He's trying to keep him calm, but it isn't working. Harrison and Gomez are in there."

Carol looks away from Joyce and up at me, then back to Joyce.

"Thanks for the warning," Joyce says.

Carol looks at her, and an awkward silence falls over the group.

"Is there anything else?" Joyce asks.

Officer Levy shakes her head and looks down, stepping aside. "No, sorry."

Joyce nods, and we walk past Carol. She opens the door, and we step inside.

The room is large, with a handful of student desks. Two larger teacher desks occupy both corners near the whiteboard at the front of the room. A young man is seated at one of the student desks. He's way too big for it. He's bent forward, his wrists cuffed behind his back, head down. His legs are crammed beneath the desk, and he looks like he might even be taller than me at six-five. His father, likely not as tall but broader, sits beside him in a chair. His hand rests on his son's shoulder. He sees us enter. Officers Harrison and Gomez stand close and nod a greeting.

Joyce walks over to the man and extends her hand. He stands as she approaches.

"Mr. Luelan, I'm Detective Joyce Powers. This is Detective Hank Gardner."

He releases her hand and takes mine. His face is calm, and I sense a gentleness about his demeanor beyond his firm grip. He's one of those men who is so big, he doesn't need a loud bark. He looks to be in his early fifties. His hair is short and flat on the top with patches of gray on the sides. The hairstyle reminds me of those old-time pictures of military men going to war.

When he releases my hand, he says, "Nice to meet you. I'm Mike Luelan. This is my son, Shawn." He pats the boy on the shoulder.

Shawn flinches but doesn't raise his head. His haircut is just like his father's. I wonder if they go to a barber or if Mike's the barber. Joyce asks him to sit back down, then angles the nearest desk so she can look directly at father and son. I don't bother with a desk and remain standing. I remember sitting at desks like these in high school. I never fit then, and there's no way I'm going to fit now. My back aches every time I see one.

"Mike," Joyce says, sitting across from him. Her eyes focus on Shawn before returning to Mike. "I wish we were meeting under better circumstances."

Mike nods. "How's Roy? Did he..." He looks away from Joyce and up at me.

I nod, and his face falls.

Joyce waits a beat before saying, "Mike, we'd like to ask Shawn some questions with your blessing. Would that be okay?"

Mike hesitates. "Does he need a lawyer? Should I be calling one?"

Joyce looks up at me, then back at Mr. Luelan. "You have every right to have one here. If you know one, feel free to call. But there really isn't any question about what happened tonight. There was a full auditorium of witnesses. We're more concerned with why it happened rather than what happened. We think Shawn might help answer that."

Shawn shifts in his seat but still doesn't look up.

Mike glances at him, debating. Finally, he looks back at Joyce and nods.

Joyce sits back in her chair and looks at Shawn. "Shawn, can you hear me?"

Shawn doesn't move.

Mike puts his hand on Shawn's back. "Shawn, buddy, these detectives want to talk to you. Can you talk to them?"

Shawn raises his head just enough to see his dad from the corner of his eye, then glances at Joyce. The boy wears a white puffy shirt and black trousers. There's blood on his sleeve.

"Shawn, can you tell me what happened tonight in the play? I hear you were Raul. Was that your name?" Joyce says.

Shawn looks up at her and nods, then puts his head back down.

"Did you sword fight with the Phantom? With Roy?"

Shawn nods again without looking up.

"Did something happen while you were fighting?"

Shawn sits still, then stands from his chair. Harrison and Gomez step forward.

Mr. Luelan tries to pull his son back down to the seat. "Shawn, sit back down, buddy."

Shawn's arms are still cuffed behind his back, but he doesn't seem to care. He steps forward, knocking over the desk. Harrison and Gomez step to him and grip either side. Shawn leans hard into Gomez, knocking him to the floor. Harrison tries to restrain him, but Shawn isn't having it and shrugs him off. He continues forward, toward the back of the classroom.

"Shawn, stop," Mr. Luelan orders, but his son isn't listening.

Shawn takes several more steps before I catch him. I grip his arms and force him to the ground. The kid is incredibly strong, and I'm not sure even I could handle him if not for his arms being restrained. When I have him on the ground, face pressed against the carpet, he screams and kicks his feet as I hold him down.

Mike tries to come over, but Gomez and Harrison stop him. Shawn turns his head and sees the two officers holding his father and screams at them. He thrashes and fights against me.

"I just want to talk to him," Mike says, holding up his hands and looking at Joyce.

Shawn continues to thrash on the floor beneath my grip, his back to me.

Joyce looks at the two officers and nods. Harrison and Gomez release him, and Mr. Luelan comes over and kneels beside his son. He puts his hand on Shawn's head and strokes it.

"Shawn, it's okay. It's going to be all right. If you just answer some of their questions, we can go home. Do you hear me? Just a couple questions, then we'll go home."

Shawn turns his head to his father and rests his cheek on the carpet. Anguish covers his expression and he sobs. "I did bad. I did it wrong," he cries.

Tears fill Mr. Luelan's eyes. "No, buddy, it's not your fault. You did just fine."

Shawn stares at his father. "Everyone hates me. Ms. Thomas is mad."

Mr. Luelan strokes Shawn's cheek. "No, buddy, you didn't do bad. Nobody is mad. It was a mistake. Only a mistake. It'll be okay."

Shawn rests his face against the ground, and huge sobs rack his body. I soften my grip as Mike rubs his back. After about a minute, Shawn's sobs lessen, and his body grows still.

Mike finally looks at me. "He doesn't understand. He doesn't know that he hurt Roy."

I stare at him, then look at Joyce. She stands with her arms crossed, watching. I motion with my head and she nods. I look at both Harrison and Gomez and wave them forward to stand guard over him. Shawn is no longer fighting. He lies dormant on the floor.

"We'll be back in a couple minutes," I say to Mr. Luelan.

Joyce and I exit the room, and when we're in the hallway with the door closed, I look at her. "What do you want to do?"

She looks at me and bites her cheek. Her gaze drops to the floor when she finally nods and says, "We'd better call the captain."

I agree and pull out my phone, dialing him, then putting the phone on speaker.

"Hank?" Captain Rigby asks when he answers.

"Hello, Captain."

"Are you still at the school?"

"We are. Joyce is with me."

I tell him everything we've learned since coming here, focusing especially on Shawn and his father. When I finish, he remains quiet on the other end of the line.

"What do you want us to do?" Joyce asks.

"I don't see how that's a question," Captain Rigby says. "This kid killed another kid in front of fifty witnesses. We've got to bring him in."

Joyce frowns. "Captain, I'm not sure he knew what he was doing. I don't think he's to blame."

"What do you mean?"

"I don't think he was trying to hurt anyone."

"Are you sure? Do you know that for certain, Detective Powers?"

Joyce looks at me.

"Listen, guys, we have no choice. We can't let a murderer just walk the streets. We have to bring him in. If he's innocent, he won't stay long."

"He's not a murderer," Joyce says.

"He isn't? I thought you said he killed that boy?"

"Killed, yes. Murder implies intent. I don't believe he had any intent."

Captain Rigby is quiet for a moment. Then, "Fine, killer. In either case, we can't allow a killer to roam our streets. The media would be all over us. Bring him in."

After we hang up, I walk back to the classroom door and open it, motioning to Mr. Luelan, asking him to join us. Shawn is back at his desk, completely subdued, his head down.

When Mike gets into the hallway, I look at Joyce, then at him. "We're going to have to take Shawn with us," I tell him.

He looks at me, then at her, panic in his eyes. "You can't."

I shake my head. "We have to."

Anger contorts his features, but he tries to control it. The tone of his voice is hard. "You can't possibly think he did this on purpose."

"We don't," Joyce says.

"Then why are you taking him to jail?"

"Whether or not he did it on purpose," I say, "he still killed someone. Until we understand more, we have to keep him in custody."

Mike looks at me, then at Joyce. The lines on his face grow softer. "Please, don't do this. It was an accident. He won't understand."

"We'll let you come with him. We'll keep him by himself. Let you stay until he's settled," I tell him.

He moves to respond, but Joyce beats him to it. "I'm sorry, Mr. Luelan. He has to come with us."

Chapter 4

Sherry

I pull the car into the garage and cut the engine before looking at my mother. I could feel her eyes on me even before I turned. Her face is covered in shadow, and the faint light from the garage door opener gleams from her glasses. I don't need to ask; I know what she's thinking.

I look in the rearview mirror at my daughter sitting in the back seat. I can barely make out her shape, her little body hunched low behind the passenger seat. She hasn't said a word since the tragedy at the school. I wonder what she knows, what she understands. She was right there, nobody closer. She watched as a boy she had gone to school with for years was stabbed to death less than ten feet away. Witness to a second violent death in less than a year.

I open the door of our Toyota Corolla and keep my eyes on her as the overhead light illuminates the interior. Nicole doesn't even blink against the light. Her eyes remain focused on the seat before her. Her expression blank.

"Honey?" When she doesn't look at me or respond, I glance at her grandma. Our eyes lock, but my mother remains silent. "Nicky, can you hear me, sweetie?"

Her gaze remains forward, her expression unchanged. I sigh and step out of the car. I'm so tired. How much more bad news can I bear? I circle the vehicle and open her door. She still doesn't move, and a lurch of panic grips me. I reach out and place a hand on her shoulder. It pulls her from her trance, and she looks up at me, eyes wide and distant.

"Honey, time to get out of the car."

She pauses before offering her hand. Her skin is cold, and I feel a tremble in her grip. With her standing beside me, I lean down and ask her to go inside while I assist her grandma. She looks at me with a blank expression before telling me she needs to go "potty."

"Okay, honey, go ahead and go."

She moves off, and I open my mother's door. I extend my hand, and she grips it. I marvel at the difference. Mother's is warm and bony. More evidence of the weight she's recently lost. It's been a month since she could exit the vehicle unassisted. With every passing day, her independence is being taken from her.

When I get her up, she stands with a hand on the door for support as I reach inside the car and withdraw her cane. I hand it to her and walk beside her into the house.

Our home is a split-entry. From the garage, you enter the house through the basement. My mother's room is on this level, along with a bathroom, laundry room, and family room. It's not a large house but enough for the three of us. When we're inside, I step around her, asking, "Are you hungry?"

She looks at me, her glasses low on her nose. I push them up for her and hear Nicole close the bathroom door at the top of the stairs. Mom thanks me, then looks longingly down the hall to the bedroom behind me. "I'm tired. I think I'll turn in for the night."

"That's not what I asked," I say with more annoyance than intended.

She turns away and walks toward her room. We had dinner before the play, but Mom didn't join us. She told me she wasn't hungry but she'd eat after the play. Her appetite has been steadily decreasing. I watch her and call out, "Let me check on Nicole, then I'll come back."

Mom ignores me, opens her bedroom door, and flips on the light while I walk up the stairs and stand outside the bathroom door, listening. The toilet flushes, and I hear Nicole walk across the bathroom to the sink. When she's done washing her hands, she opens the door and sees me standing at the top of the stairs.

I'm not tall, only five feet four inches, but Nicole is exceptionally short. Although she's technically an adult, being eighteen, she's less than four and a half feet tall, and mentally the age of a seven-year-old.

"Are you ready to get to bed?" I ask her.

She looks down the dark hallway toward her room, then back to me. "Can I color?"

The question catches me by surprise. She's always enjoyed coloring children's books but never at night. Nicole is a person who loves structure and struggles anytime the structure is broken. At night, she typically watches her TV shows, like *Sesame Street* or *Mister Rogers' Neighborhood*. On the weekends, she watches her favorite movies, like *The Princess Bride*.

"Don't you think it's a little late for coloring? Look outside; it's dark."

She looks down the darkened hallway, then back at me. "Just for a little bit?"

I think about what she's been through today, and although I'm tired and want a break, I agree, but only if she puts on her pajamas first. I flip on the hallway light, and she goes to her room while I go to the kitchen and make my mother a peanut butter sandwich. Just as I'm ready to take it to her, Nicole enters the kitchen wearing her Minnie Mouse pajamas and carrying her coloring books and crayons. As she arranges them on the table, I tell her I'll be back and go downstairs carrying the sandwich on a plate and holding a glass of milk.

When I enter my mother's room, I see she's undressed but has given up trying to dress herself and sits on the end of the bed with her pajama bottoms at her ankles.

"I'm sorry," she says.

"For what?" I ask and help her stand. I pull up the pants and help with her shirt. It buttons in the front, and she sits back down while I fasten each button.

"How is she?" Mother asks.

"She wanted to color," I say, and reach behind me to the dresser where I placed the sandwich and milk. I hold them in both hands and motion for Mother to take the sandwich.

"I said I wasn't hungry."

"No, you said you were tired. You never said you weren't hungry. You have to eat."

She looks at me, then grabs the sandwich. She takes a small bite, then puts it back.

"I want more than that."

She chews, then gives me a look. "She doesn't color at night."

I nod as she picks up the sandwich and takes another bite. After chewing, she takes a drink of milk, then waves me away. I'm eager to return to Nicole and don't have the energy to argue. I help her into bed, but before I can leave, she clears her throat.

"Sherry. You need to talk to her."

I nod and pick up the plate and cup, then turn out the lights and close the door. I walk up the stairs. I know she's right. At least, I know that's what the experts say. Talk it out. Communicate. But they don't know what we've been through. They don't know how difficult it'll be for her. Nicole isn't able to communicate her feelings like a normal teenager. For months after her father's death, she drew deeper within herself. Every time I tried to talk to her about it, she seemed to get worse. Not to mention the seizures. It was easier not to talk about it.

I knew better than anyone how much she loved her father, but she never showed any grief. It was impossible to know what she understood. She was a statue. Even at his funeral, she never cried. I don't think she knew how. Her pain remained beneath the surface. She missed him, was struggling with the loss, but no matter what I did, I couldn't seem to reach her.

They say time heals all wounds, and I don't think I've seen a better example than her. At first, she coped by staying busy. She'd color constantly, always with a single crayon. Then one day, I saw more colors. Red and yellow and blue left the box. She was returning to her normal routine. She started listening to her music and watching her movies. She was going to be okay.

I reach the top of the stairs, smile at her as she sits at the table, focused on her picture. I cross the kitchen to the sink and pour out the milk, then throw out the sandwich and wash the dishes. When I go to the table, preparing to sit beside her, I stop, seeing the color she holds in her hand. The page is full of it. She's reverted to who she was following her father's death. The page is nothing but black.

Chapter 5
Hank

I sit in the Dodge Charger and watch as the front door to Joyce's house opens. She's standing in the doorframe, saying something to her husband. I wish she'd hurry. It's beginning to snow, and I don't want it to stick before we get to the station. Her little dog, Jack Jack, is bouncing up and down behind the screen door. What kind of dog is he? Some kind of terrier or something.

She finally exits and walks down the steps. She gives me a look before getting in the car.

"What?" I say as she climbs in.

She says nothing.

I put the car in reverse and pull out of the driveway. Joyce stares out the window as if she doesn't have a care in the world. Who am I kidding? She's always got something on her mind.

"What was that look?" I ask more forcefully.

She turns to me with a half-smile but still says nothing.

I turn right onto S Boulevard and feel the tires slip on the freezing surface. My anxiety rises, and I grip the steering wheel tighter. Even though I've lived in Idaho for almost nine years, I'm still not completely comfortable driving in snowy conditions. Joyce points at the dash, and I shoot her a curious look.

"You didn't change the station."

"What?"

"On the radio. You didn't change the station after you dropped me off."

I frown. "What are you talking about?"

"I watched you as I came out of the house. Every time since we became partners, you've changed the radio station when I'm not in the vehicle. This time you didn't. Why?"

I turn onto Northgate Mile, and the back tires spin before grabbing. Why would they give us a rear-wheel drive car in Idaho? The snow falls in large flakes, and I turn up the windshield wipers.

"I didn't?"

She shakes her head.

"Maybe I had the case on my mind," I say, looking at the road. "I wasn't listening."

"Nope," she says, giving me a look and shaking her head.

I sigh. "What then?"

There's that smile. "You like my music."

I chuckle and pull into the parking lot. The space lines are covered with snow. But it doesn't matter. Our car is the only one in front of the building.

"Do you deny it?"

I shut off the car and turn to her. "You think I'd rather listen to your hair bands than my Cali rap?"

"I didn't say that. I said you like my music."

I shake my head and roll my eyes. "Come on. Let's get in there before the snow swallows us whole."

"It's just a couple of flakes," she says as she climbs out of the car.

I get out and nearly slip, walking up to the front door of the police station. Joyce holds the door for me, and we go inside, stomping our feet. When I reach my cubicle, I remove my coat and hang it on the back of my chair. Joyce is in the cubicle next to me, and I can already hear her typing on her computer. I look over the cubicle and peek at her screen. She's leaning over her desk.

"What are you doing?"

"I just want to check something real quick."

She moves the mouse and angles the screen away from me. I give her a curious look, but she doesn't see it. After a second, she straightens, and we walk toward the interrogation room.

Captain Rigby stands talking to Officer Levy in the hallway. He sees us coming and holds up a hand to her. The captain is a tall man, an inch or two over six feet. I've been told he was lean at one time, although I have a hard time picturing it. He has a handlebar mustache, and the light gleams off his bald head.

"Gardner, Powers," he says as we approach.

"Captain," I say.

Joyce looks at him, saying nothing.

The captain motions with his head. "He's not in there."

I look at the light streaming below the door and frown.

He looks at Levy. "When we were bringing," she hesitates, searching for the word, "the special kid—"

Joyce bristles. "Shawn or Mr. Luelan would be fine. He has a name, Officer."

Levy nods, then shakes her head, looking down. "Right. When we were bringing Mr. Luelan to the station, he had an episode."

I frown at her. "What kind?"

Levy looks at Captain Rigby, then back up at me. "He freaked out. Started hyperventilating in the back of the car. He passed out."

"Where is he now?" Joyce asks.

"We had Dr. Shepard check him out. The boy is fine. The doctor gave him something to calm him. He's sleeping now in one of the cells."

"And his father is in there?" Joyce says, motioning toward the closed door.

Captain Rigby nods. "He wants to talk to the two of you. I told him we have to keep his son until we get a better handle on all this, but he wants to hear it from you. I guess the police captain isn't enough."

Joyce turns toward the door and rolls her eyes, then looks back at the captain.

"I agree with him," she says. "The boy should be allowed to go home."

Captain Rigby straightens and puffs out his chest. "That's my call, Detective. Not yours."

Joyce shrugs. "You're wrong."

Levy takes a step away from Captain Rigby, and the captain looks at her. "Don't you have somewhere you need to be, Levy?"

"Yes, sir," she says, turning and nearly running down the hall.

Captain Rigby drops his voice when she's beyond earshot, but his tone is hard and firm. "Detective Powers, I give you latitude because you get results. But if you ever contradict me again in front of another officer, I'll suspend you so fast your badge will be nothing but a memory. Do you understand me?"

"Hank's always with me," she says.

"Gardner is different. But I don't like it in front of him either."

Joyce gives him a look like she's bored with the conversation, and I almost shrink back in fear, worrying about her next words. But they never come. She only nods and walks toward the interview room door, opening it. I glance at Captain Rigby and see he's just as surprised as I am. He watches her, open-mouthed. Joyce glances back at me, wanting me to follow. She holds the door, allowing me to go first. As I pass her, she winks out of sight of Rigby.

Inside the room, Mr. Luelan sits behind the table on the opposite side. His arms are crossed, and the muscles in his face are tight. I don't have to talk to him to know emotion is running high in this room. I pull two seats up along the opposite side of the table while Joyce shuts the door and joins me.

Joyce looks at me, and I turn back to Mr. Luelan.

"You wanted to speak with us?"

He pushes his seat back and leans forward, resting his elbows on his knees. He's such a thick man; the effect makes him look broader. "This isn't right." He looks from me to Joyce. "You know that."

"What isn't right?" I say.

"Shawn being here. He didn't mean to hurt anyone. It was an accident. It was negligence on the part of Georgette Thomas. She's the one who should be here. Not Shawn."

"Shawn's teacher?" Joyce asks.

He nods. "How could they have let those boys use actual swords? If I had known, I would never have allowed it. Shawn," he pauses and shakes his head, looking down, "he's such an innocent kid. Sometimes he doesn't understand his size and strength." He looks up at me. "You know what I mean?"

I do. I flash back to my junior year at Covina High in Southern California. I rushed the passer, and the left tackle missed the block. I can still hear the crack of the bones as I landed on top of the quarterback. When I got up, I remember his screams of pain. I looked down and saw a bone sticking out from his football pants. It still haunts me.

He straightens and leans back in the chair. "You've got to let him go," he says to Joyce. "He doesn't understand. If you keep him in here, it'll kill him."

I watch him, but my attention is on Joyce. I wait, eager for what she might say.

"I'm sorry, Mr. Luelan. Until we know more, Shawn has to stay. I suggest you call a lawyer. Maybe they can help you."

Chapter 6
Sherry

I pull the car into the parking spot at Skyline High School and turn off the engine. When I look back, Nicole sits motionless, staring at the back of the passenger seat. She's said very little since leaving the school last night and coloring with only a black crayon. I get out of the car and come around to her side and open the door. She still doesn't move, and I set my hand on her shoulder.

"Honey, are you ready to go inside?"

She stares at me with a blank face. "Yes," she says, getting out of the car, taking her red backpack from me. I wish I knew what was going on in her mind. She holds my hand as we walk along the path to the front doors.

Early this morning, I called the school and spoke with her teacher, Ms. Thomas. I told her Nicole wouldn't be riding the bus today. I asked if we could have a conference, and she suggested we meet with the principal and the school counselor at ten.

We enter through the front doors, and I feel Nicole's grip tighten. The head office is to our right, where the school secretary greets us. Mr. Roberts, the school counselor, sits in one chair, sipping a cup of coffee. He notices us enter but doesn't greet us. He's a slovenly fellow, and I don't care for him. The secretary points us to a couple of chairs beside him and tells us the principal will be with us shortly. We sit, and I notice Mr. Roberts is watching us while holding his coffee cup to his lips.

I turn away from him and smile at Nicole. She's eighteen and in her senior year, yet her feet can't reach the ground while sitting in an adult chair. They dangle as she holds her backpack in her lap. She's not looking at me or anyone else. Her gaze is distant. I wonder what she's thinking. Is she scared? Is she confused? Why did she only use black while coloring? Is that some sort of psychological coping mechanism? I didn't understand it after her father's accident, and I don't understand it now. When I tried to make her change colors, she gave me a look I'll never forget. It was nothing short of terror.

A girl, probably Nicole's age, enters the office. She's tall and lean with beautiful, long, straight hair and dark eyelashes. I wonder if they're fake. She walks toward the secretary, then stops when she sees us. She changes direction and nearly skips to Nicole's side.

"Nicole. Hi," she says, kneeling before her. "How are you doing? Are you okay?" She reaches out and rubs Nicole's hand, frowning with concern.

Nicole looks up into her eyes, and I see recognition. She smiles for the first time since she was onstage last night. The girl smiles back, then glances at me and winks. She pats Nicole's backpack. "What do you have in there? Do you have your Oakridge Boys CDs?"

Nicole nods enthusiastically and begins opening the backpack. I consider stopping her, we're about to go into a meeting. But I think of what she's been through, and I'm so pleased to see her smile.

I can't remember the exact moment, but for as long as I can remember, Nicole has adored the Oakridge Boys, a country-western band from Oakridge, Tennessee. Something about the group of four men triggered a response within her, and she was hooked. Their music is all she listens to, though I've tried to get her to branch out. Several years ago, I gave her an old iPhone and loaded their music on it, but she struggled to make it work. She likes to see the CDs and show off the covers. A Discman makes more sense for her. I only hope it never breaks. If it does, I don't know how I'll replace it.

Nicole proudly withdraws the Discman and offers the headphones to the girl. She takes them, and Nicole presses play and giggles as the girl bobs her head to the music. The girl looks at me and winks as I feel my eyes fill with tears.

After several seconds, the door opens again, and Georgette Thomas, Nicole's special education teacher, enters. She greets the secretary, then angles toward us. She's a willow of a woman, slender, with a permanent frown on her face. I secretly refer to her as "Permacrust." I stand and shake her hand, thanking her for the meeting. She nods, then looks at the girl and Nicole. She pats the girl on the shoulder and motions for her to remove the headphones.

"Mindy, shouldn't you be in class right now?"

Mindy looks taken aback. "I came down because I was called to the office. When I saw Nicole, I thought it was to help her." She stands, and she's several inches taller than Ms. Thomas.

"Did you ask Mrs. Wallace? I highly doubt that's why you've been called down here."

The girl hands the headphones back to Nicole and walks to the secretary. Georgette watches her for a moment, then turns back to Nicole.

"Nicole, I've told you before, you can't take your CDs out of your backpack unless I say you can. Do you want them taken away again?"

Nicole shakes her head and quickly stuffs the Discman back into her backpack, closing the zipper. Ms. Thomas watches her, then turns to me.

"I think it would be best if Nicole weren't at this meeting, don't you? She can go to class with her fellow students. Ms. Ferguson will be here shortly to see that she makes it safely."

Before I can respond, the principal's office door opens, and Principal Skinner comes striding out. He's wearing a blue suit, a blue shirt, and a brown tie. The wrinkles around his mouth look more pronounced than I've seen them in the past. Seymour is a longtime friend of our family. He and my husband grew up together on the same street. He spoke at his funeral.

He extends his hand, but before I take it, his attention is pulled away. A blood-curdling scream pierces the air. I know that sound all too well. Nicole has begun seizing beside me. She releases the backpack, and it falls to the ground as she shakes uncontrollably. It seems strange to say, but seizures have become a common occurrence for us. As long as she's seated or lying down, she can't hurt herself.

I turn and grip her body, supporting her as she convulses in a rigid state. Drool oozes from her mouth, and her eyes roll back in her head. After several seconds, the shaking slows, then stops. Her eyes shut, and she snores loudly. I roll her to her side, positioning her on the chair, making sure she can't roll off. When I'm done, I look up to see the other people in the room all staring at her, wide-eyed.

"Is she okay?" Principal Skinner asks.

I look past him and see that the secretary, Mrs. Wallace, is on the phone. She's called emergency services and is requesting an ambulance. Before I can tell her to stop, Ms. Thomas spins around and walks toward her.

"Mrs. Wallace, hang up that phone. She's fine. We don't need an ambulance."

Mrs. Wallace holds the phone to her ear, open-mouthed and looking at Principal Skinner. Georgette leans over the counter and takes the phone from her. She tells the person on the other end of the phone to cancel the ambulance. After several seconds of explanation, she hangs up and walks back to us.

"This happens sometimes," Georgette says. "Things get a little overwhelming for her, and she does this. She'll sleep for a few minutes, then have no memory of it."

Nicole's head rests in my lap, and her snoring has become lighter. I look up at them, knowing I can't move her.

"Would it be okay if we met here instead?"

Georgette pulls a chair to face me. Mr. Skinner and Mr. Roberts look at each other, then follow suit. We huddle in a circle in the corner of the main office while Nicole sits in a chair, her head in my lap.

We all wait, letting Mr. Skinner take the lead. He looks at me, then at her.

"Are you sure you still want to meet?"

I nod.

"Okay, yes, well, thank you for coming to meet us today, Mrs. Morgan. I'm very glad you made this appointment. We appreciate it. And let me just say, what happened last night was a devastating tragedy. A shock to all of us."

He looks at Ms. Thomas, then at Mr. Roberts, for confirmation. They both look at me and nod with grave expressions.

"We want to assure you, we take student safety very seriously. We don't have all the facts yet. The police are still investigating, but every student's safety is our top priority."

I look at him, then at the other two administrators, and realize he's trying to save his job. A student was killed by another student last night at the school. I thought I was the one setting this meeting, but it's clear they want it most. They wanted to meet with me to assure me Nicole is safe so I won't go to the district—or worse.

They wait expectantly. I thought I was making the appointment to talk about Nicole, but they had other motivations.

"How did it happen?" I ask.

Mr. Skinner looks down and straightens his tie. "That's still under investigation."

I frown. "So, you don't know?"

He looks at the other two.

"No," Georgette says.

Nicole stirs and opens her eyes. She pushes up and sits in the chair, looking at me with a blank face. I rub her shoulder and smile. "How are you doing, honey?"

She frowns, then moves her jaw back and forth like someone in the movies who has just been punched. She slouches in the chair, then sees her backpack and picks it up, holding it to her. With her awake now and realizing this meeting is no longer about her, I get an urge to leave.

"Well, until you know and can guarantee my daughter's safety, she won't be coming back to school." I turn back to Nicole. "Do you want to go home?"

She looks at me and nods.

I stand and grip her hand, helping her up and guiding her from the office.

Chapter 7
Hank

It's morning, and I'm back in the Charger waiting for Joyce. We're getting a later start than usual. Last night, after investigating the murder and talking with Mr. Luelan, we didn't go home. We had paperwork to file and conversations to have. Neither of us wanted to leave until we had a plan. It was after two before we finally called it a night.

A commercial comes on the radio, and I turn the station. After pressing two options, I stop at 101. Yesterday, Joyce caught me listening to this station, even when she wasn't in the car. It's not the first time. The words are familiar, and I start singing along while thumping on the steering wheel.

With the lights out, it's less dangerous
Here we are now, entertain us
I feel stupid and contagious
Here we are now, entertain us

The front door of Joyce's house opens, and she steps onto the porch. When she turns around to lock the door, I reach forward and change the station back to Z103. I recognize the song. It's about thirty years newer than the one I was just listening to, "Luther" by Kendrick Lamar.

Joyce walks down the steps and opens the door. A rush of cold air sweeps into the car.

"New coat?" I ask as she reaches for her seat belt.

She fastens the belt and looks at me. "Do you like it?"

I put the car in reverse and look her up and down. "It's nice. North Face?"

"Yeah."

She pulls the hood down over her head and rubs the material. "I don't know about this fur in the hood."

I pull onto the street, and she frowns at the radio in the dash. "What is this?" She reaches forward and changes the channel back to the station I had it on before. The Nirvana song ended, and a new song is playing. She doesn't know it, but I'd rather be listening to this.

There is no blame, only shame
When you beg, you just complain
The more I come, more I try
All police are paranoid

"For a Coke?" she says, pointing to the radio.

I look at her and sigh, turning back to the road. "Hmm," I say, chewing on my cheek. "I want to say Live, but I know it's not them." I rub my chin while steering with the other hand. I see from the corner of my eye, she's watching me. I'm about to answer, but she beats me to it.

"Never mind," she says and turns away from me.

I look at her. "What?"

She doesn't look at me, keeping her attention out the window at the piles of snow lining the street. "I withdraw the question. The bet is off."

"You can't do that."

She looks at me. "Why can't I?"

"It's 'Comedown' by Bush."

"Good job. But I'm not buying you a Coke."

"You have to," I say, turning right onto Pancheri Drive and crossing over I-15.

"No, I don't." She pretends to be driving the car and rubs her chin with her hand. "Hmm, well, I know it's not Live," she says in an exaggerated deep voice.

I burst out laughing. She slaps my shoulder and shakes her head as I pull into the school parking lot.

"You still owe me a Coke," I say as we walk up to the front doors.

"How do you figure?"

"The bet is whether or not I know the song. I knew the song, even if I played like I didn't."

A woman exits the doors several paces ahead. She's holding a girl's hand. The girl has short, dark hair and is short but looks older than a middle school or elementary student. As they pass, Joyce watches her as well.

When they're out of earshot, Joyce looks at me. "Do you think she's special needs?"

I nod. "The mother didn't look happy."

"Hmm," she says.

We watch them walk out to the parking lot and get in their car. When they're gone, we enter the school. The principal's office is in the front of the building. We've been here before. A woman sits behind the desk but doesn't seem to recognize us.

"Can I help you?"

"Yes," I say. "We'd like to talk with Principal Skinner."

We hold out our badges, and the woman examines them, her eyes widening with recognition. "You've been here before."

I nod.

"Wait just a minute. You can have a seat over there." She points to a group of chairs across the room that are arranged in a circle just outside the principal's office.

We follow her instructions and sit in the chairs. A low rumble of voices can be heard from behind the door. After three minutes, the door opens, and a man and a woman exit. I recognize the man. He's the school's guidance counselor. We talked to him in another case several months back. They leave the office, and Skinner comes out and sees us waiting.

"Can I help you?"

"Sir," the secretary nearly shouts from the other side of the room, "they're police."

He holds up a hand. "I know. Thank you, Brenda." He extends a hand to us, shaking mine first, then Joyce's. "Come into my office," he says, ushering us inside. He walks around the desk while we sit in the chairs opposite him. The seat is still warm from his last meeting. "Something tells me you're not here about broken lockers."

We weren't last time either. Broken lockers were a byproduct of our investigation. Not a cause.

"I think you know why we're here," I say.

He exhales and looks down at his desk. "Tragic what happened last night. I've been dealing with it all day. I just don't know how something like that could have happened. I can't imagine anything worse."

I can, but I don't say it. "You don't have any idea how it happened?"

He shakes his head. "None."

I frown. "We were hoping you would. No clues? Guesses?"

Skinner folds his hands on the desk. "That's what I was just talking with Ms. Thomas about. She's their teacher and play director. She said she didn't know how the sword got onstage. The one they had was wooden but painted silver to look more realistic, just like the metal one."

I glance at Joyce. She's looking at the bookcase along the wall.

"Wooden?" I say, bumping Joyce with my elbow. She glares at me.

He leans back in his chair. "Of course. We would never have allowed those boys to use metal swords."

"But only one was metal," Joyce says, still not looking at him.

He looks at her, then follows her eyes to the bookcase. "Right. Neither sword was supposed to be metal. They were both supposed to be wooden. Even then, Ms. Thomas worried they might hurt each other. At first, they practiced with toy swords, but everything went fine, and she felt comfortable with wood. They looked more realistic."

Joyce looks back at me.

"Where were you when it happened?" I ask.

Principal Skinner picks up the stapler on his desk and passes it from hand to hand. "In the back of the auditorium. I was controlling the lights. One of the kids from the class was responsible, but he had to go."

"Go?"

"To the bathroom."

Joyce sits forward. "One of the kids from the class who was operating the lights left during the performance?"

Skinner nods. "I was staying close to the control panel since the other teachers were involved in directing the play. I wasn't expecting to be needed, but I was there just in case."

"Did you notice anyone else leave the auditorium around that same time?" Joyce asks.

He shakes his head.

"What is the name of the student who handled the lighting?"

Skinner puts his fingers to his lips and looks up. "Ty Malone."

"Is Ty...in the special class?"

Skinner nods.

I make a note on my notepad, then look at Joyce. She's still watching Skinner. I cross my arms and look at him. "I want to go back to my previous question. How do you think this happened last night?"

Skinner swivels his chair to the side and looks away from me. He's leaning back in the chair, staring at the brick wall. "I think Shawn Luelan brought the sword with him. My guess is he felt the wooden swords weren't realistic enough, and he brought the metal sword to make it seem more real." He looks at me. "You know, some of these kids are just so innocent. Childlike. I don't think Shawn meant to hurt anyone."

I nod and glance at Joyce. She's looking at me. I've worked with her long enough to know what that means.

"Thank you, Principal Skinner. Would it be possible for us to talk with the teachers and perhaps some of the students?" I ask.

"Is that legal?" he asks.

"Perfectly. At least the teachers. Some of the underage students will need their parents' permission. But that's only if we treat them like suspects."

Skinner nods, looking at the clock on the wall. "Lunch starts in a few minutes. Where would you like to start?"

"How about the teacher, Ms. Thomas? The play director."

"Okay." He stands and walks to the door. Joyce calls out to him before he opens it.

"Mr. Skinner, have you ever been to Japan?"

Skinner gives her a curious look. "Japan?"

"Yes, the island in Asia. Have you been there?"

He shakes his head.

"Have you known anyone who has? Anyone here at the school, perhaps?"

"Um...I'm not sure. I can't think of any. Why?"

Joyce shrugs. "Just curious."

Chapter 8
Hank

As we exit the office with Principal Skinner, the bell rings, and within seconds, the hallways are jammed with teenagers. The sounds of laughter, yelling, and conversation fill the narrow walkways. At first, the three of us walk side by side but have to adjust to single file as the pathways become narrower. Skinner is lean and about five inches shorter than me, but still six feet tall and easy to follow. Joyce, on the other hand, is a foot shorter than I am and is dwarfed by many of the students.

"Hi, Principal Skinner," a girl says as she passes with two friends.

"Katy," he says, nodding in her direction.

The girls giggle at each other, and I find the interaction curious.

We round a corner, and this hallway is a little less crowded. A group of boys stands against a row of lockers. Each is wearing Wrangler jeans and cowboy boots. Most have a large buckle on their belts. They look like they're ready to audition for a part in a rodeo movie. They form a half circle, joking and laughing about something, when a boy wearing a Spider-Man shirt passes by. He's holding a binder and two books and nervously looks in their direction. One cowboy sees him and hits his friend, nodding and grinning. The friend picks up the cue and pushes the cowboy into the small boy. The boy bounces off and falls, sliding across the hallway into the legs of a group of girls. His books and binder spray out all over the floor.

"Keith!" Skinner yells.

He grabs the large cowboy and pulls him away from the boy. Joyce goes to the small boy and helps him up while Skinner holds the cowboy by the wrist as he tries to free himself.

"Come with me," Skinner scolds.

"What? I didn't do anything. We were just screwing around. It was an accident."

Skinner scowls at him. "You don't think I saw that?" He looks at us. Joyce has the boy up, and I've picked up his books and binder and am giving them back to him. "I'm taking him to the office. Ms. Thomas's room is up ahead, two doors on the left. Is he okay?"

The smaller boy nods with his head down, gathering his books and binder from us.

Skinner turns away and speaks to the rest of the group of cowboys. "Next time I see anything like this, I'll suspend all of you."

The group of boys just stare at him. As Skinner walks away with Keith, one of them comments on how Skinner got a flagpole stuck up his butt early that morning. They all laugh, and one of them pantomimes sticking something up his rear. I look at Joyce and see the small boy is gone, and she's watching the group of cowboys. She looks at me and raises an eyebrow, and I wonder if she's thinking the same thing I am. Boy, am I glad to be done with high school.

I take a step in the direction Skinner told us but stop when I see Joyce isn't joining me. She's crossing the hall, approaching the group of cowboys.

"Tommy," she says in a whiny voice.

The boy who made the comment about the flagpole turns and looks at her.

"Tommy, your mommy sent me. I'm your Auntie Joannie. Remember me?"

Tommy looks at her in bewilderment.

"You remember, don't you? I gave you that Hannah Montana poster you liked so much."

His face instantly colors, and he shakes his head. "I don't have—"

"Oh, it's okay, Tommy. Remember, you said you were going to marry her someday?"

The boy closest to Tommy bursts out laughing and puts his hand over his mouth. Tommy looks at him, then back at Joyce.

"I got you some more of those Hulk underwear you like so much. I have to go back to Pocatello, but I wanted to see you. Give me a hug before I go."

Joyce reaches for him, but he backs away. He scowls at her and motions for his friends to follow. When they're down the hall, he looks back one more time before turning the corner.

Joyce looks at me and winks, and we continue up the hall and enter Ms. Thomas's room. Ms. Thomas sits behind the desk in the corner. The rest of the room is empty. She's looking at the computer and doesn't see us enter. I clear my throat, and she looks up.

"Yes?"

"Ms. Thomas?"

"Yes?"

"Hi, we're detectives with the IFPD," I say.

"Oh," she says, pulling off her glasses and setting them on the desk.

We hold up our badges as we approach. She examines them, then looks back up at me.

"Am I in trouble?" she asks.

"Do you want to be?" I ask. She gives me a look and I smile. "Just a little joke. We'd like to ask you a few questions. We're investigating what happened last night at the play and thought you might be able to help us."

She nods and motions for us to sit at the desks closest to her. Joyce sits in one, but I know if I try to squeeze myself into the other, I'm going to be wearing it. An image of me standing with a desk connected to my body flashes through my mind. I look around and see a chair against the wall. I walk over, grab it, and place it beside Joyce.

When I'm seated, Ms. Thomas looks at me and asks, "Is Shawn okay?"

I blow out my breath. "He's struggling."

She looks down and taps her finger on the glass surface, sighing. "I just...I don't know how it happened. How did I not see it?"

"See what?" I ask.

"That it was a real sword."

"Will you walk us through it?" Joyce asks.

Ms. Thomas looks at Joyce and bites her cheek. "We've been practicing the play for a couple months. Roy, the boy who…" She stops and places her hand on her chest. When she speaks, it's in a subdued tone. "The boy who died. He loved *The Phantom of the Opera*." She stops and looks up. "Have you been around many special-needs kids? Either of you?"

We shake our heads.

She nods. "Not always, but many fixate on things that make them feel comfortable. Not unlike all of us. Some people have vacations they take in the same place every year. Some watch the same movies over and over. Some have comfort foods or drinks. I've found that many of my students gravitate to music. Nicole, for instance, loves the Oakridge Boys."

"Who?" Joyce asks.

"Nicole."

"No, I mean, what was that band name? I assume it's a band."

"Yes, the Oakridge Boys. They're a country-western band. Shawn, who you know, loves Elvis Presley. Roy loved *The Phantom of the Opera*. He'd wear Phantom shirts and even had a mask in his backpack that we wouldn't let him wear. But knowing he loved the music and had the lyrics memorized, we thought it would be fun to allow him to perform the play this year."

"You do a play each year?" I ask.

She nods. "Roy was the obvious choice for the Phantom. He knew all the songs before we even started practicing. He had Down syndrome, but he was high-functioning. The highest in the class, actually. He was the natural choice for the lead. Plus, he already had the mask."

"Is that why you chose that play?" I ask.

"What do you mean?"

I shrug. "Well, it's December. Why not something holiday-themed?"

She frowns. "I let the kids choose. They chose Phantom of the Opera."

"How many kids do you have in your class?" Joyce asks.

"Five. I know that doesn't seem like very many, but believe me, it's a lot."

"What are their names?" I ask, notepad and pen in hand.

"Roy Edwards, the Phantom. He…"

"Right. He's the one who passed," I say.

"Then there's Shawn, who you know. He played Raul. Nicole, who played Christine. Marilyn, who played Madame Giri, and Ty Malone."

"Who did he play?" I ask.

"He didn't want to star in the play. He wanted to run the lights, so we let him. He saw himself as the producer."

"How did you do *Phantom of the Opera* with so few characters?" Joyce asks.

She looks back at Joyce. "It wasn't the full version. It was the highlights. We couldn't do the full version. Plus, it was challenging to do as much as we did. The whole thing was only scheduled for twenty minutes."

"When did the sword fight take place? How far in?" Joyce asks.

"About halfway."

I make a note, and Joyce looks across the room. "I see another teacher's desk. You team teach?"

She nods. "Lucrezia Ferguson is the other teacher."

"Where is she?"

Georgette puts her finger to her lips. "She called out today. She was really upset last night. She was especially close to Roy."

Joyce and I look at each other.

"So, last night," Joyce says, "where were you when the incident happened? What was going on?"

"I was backstage helping Marilyn. Madame Giri."

"With what?" Joyce asks.

Ms. Thomas takes a deep breath. "Marilyn wanted to leave."

"Leave?" I ask.

She holds up a hand. "Yes. But that's not unusual for her. She gets," she pauses, searching for the word, "upset easily. She made a mistake in her earlier part and didn't want to go back on. I was encouraging her during the sword fight. My back was to the stage."

"So, you didn't see it happen?" Joyce asks.

"No."

"I understand both swords were supposed to be wooden. Is that right?"

"Yes."

"Do you have any idea how a metal sword got onstage? How did it go unnoticed?"

She sighs and puts her knuckles to her teeth. Her hand is trembling with the memory. "I didn't even think to look at the swords.

I remember seeing them earlier, when we were setting up, and they looked normal. That was the last thing on my mind."

"Both looked wooden?" Joyce asks.

"Well, I don't know that for certain. I mean, they looked like the swords we'd been using. I didn't hold them. I just saw them leaning against a wall backstage."

"Who had access to the swords? Where did they come from?" I ask.

"They were a donation by a member of the community." A school bell rings, and she looks up at the clock above the door. Noise in the hallway increases. "Um...the kids will be coming back. Lunch is over. I've got to prepare."

She stands, and Joyce and I thank her. I turn toward the door, but Joyce remains still.

"Ms. Thomas?" Joyce says.

"Yes?"

"Would you mind if we stayed for a few minutes to observe the class? We'll keep to the back, out of the way."

She shrugs. "That's fine."

We walk to the back of the room and stand beside the wall near the windows. Less than thirty seconds later, another woman enters. She looks at us, then at Ms. Thomas, before continuing to the desk in the other corner. She must be a substitute. Ms. Thomas goes to the whiteboard and writes something at the top. After several more seconds, students come into the room. Each is accompanied by another student from the general student body. It's only one boy and one girl. Someone is missing, and I think about the small girl who left the front doors of the school this morning with her mother.

I look over at Joyce and see she's noticed the same thing. Only two kids sit at desks. The two other kids, the ones who accompanied the students with special needs, stay for only a few seconds and then leave. Both glance over at us on their way out.

"How was lunch?" Ms. Thomas asks the students.

The boy, Ty, I assume, gives a thumbs-up. He's tapping his fingers on his desk like he's playing the drums. The girl, either Marilyn or Nicole, has her head down and seems upset.

"Marilyn," Ms. Thomas says. "What's wrong?"

Marilyn puts her head down on the desk and starts to cry. Ms. Thomas looks at Ty.

"She doesn't like mashed potatoes," Ty says.

Ms. Thomas nods, then moves over to Marilyn and talks to her.

We stay in the room for fifteen minutes, then quietly exit. Before leaving the building, we stop back by the head office. A young girl sits behind the desk. The secretary, who helped us earlier, sits staring at a computer behind her. The principal's office door is closed.

"Can I help you?" the young girl asks.

"Yes," Joyce says, not looking at her but at the woman in the background, "where is Nicole Morgan today?"

The woman stands and comes over to the desk. "Her mother took her out of school today."

Joyce nods. "Is she sick?"

The woman shakes her head, then leans forward, dropping her voice. "She met with Principal Skinner, Ms. Thomas, and Mr.

Roberts. I don't think she was happy with the meeting and left. She took Nicole with her."

Joyce thanks her, and we walk out of the office.

When we reach the car, I look at Joyce. "Where to next?"

"Let's go back to the jail. I have an idea."

Chapter 9
Sherry

After I pull the car into the garage, I adjust the rearview mirror so I can look at Nicole. She's retreated within herself again. For a few minutes, I saw the girl she used to be while talking with Mindy and showing her CDs. Now she's back to staring at the seat in front of her, her eyes vacant. I turn so I can see her better. She doesn't blink or move.

"Hey," I say.

For several seconds, she doesn't react. Finally, her eyes focus on me and I smile.

"Are you hungry?"

She shakes her head.

"Thirsty?"

Again, she shakes her head. We watch each other.

"Should we go inside?"

She looks toward the house. "Mom?"

"Yes?"

"Can I watch Sesee?"

Sesee is short for *Sesame Street*. Every day after school, she goes to her room and watches *Sesame Street* while I prepare dinner.

"I'm not sure it's on yet, honey."

She stares at me with confusion in her eyes.

"Remember, we left the school early today. We're home earlier than normal."

She frowns and looks down.

"What about *The Princess Bride*? Would you like to watch that?"

She looks up with excitement. "Okay," she says and reaches for the door handle.

I get out and walk around to her side, but she's already out of the car and reaching for her backpack on the seat. She looks up at me and smiles, and I rest my hand on her shoulder as we walk into the house.

"Mom," I call from the bottom of the stairs. "We're home."

I hear a muffled response from the bedroom down the hall.

"I need to go potty," Nicole says.

"Okay, honey. Go on up. I'm going to check on your grandma."

Nicole goes up the stairs, and I walk down the hall and open Mother's door. She's still in bed, the remote control in her hand. She pauses the TV as she leans on an elbow, and I notice an old man with white hair on the screen wearing a silver suit and standing in a courtroom.

"You doing okay?" I ask her.

"Fine."

"Have you been out of bed yet?"

"I got myself to the little girls' room."

"Did you eat anything?"

She gives me a look.

"What?"

"Are you writing a book?"

"Why won't you answer me?"

She hits play on the remote, and the old man talks.

"Mom?"

She doesn't look at me.

"Mom, you need your strength. You need to eat."

She shakes her head and shushes me.

"Mom, how many times have you watched *Matlock*? I can just glance at the screen and know which episode this is."

She presses pause and looks at me. "Sherry, why do you ask questions you already know the answer to?"

I hear water running down the pipes in the wall and know Nicole is finishing upstairs.

"I'm going to get Nicole set on her TV, then you're eating something."

She looks away from me while nodding and presses play.

I walk upstairs and find Nicole standing in the kitchen, waiting for me. She's looking at me, but her eyes aren't focused. I wish I could get inside her head and know what she's thinking. What set her off at the school today?

"Nicki?"

She looks at me.

"*The Princess Bride*?"

She smiles, and we walk down the hall to her room. She sits in her chair as I set up the DVD player with her movie. I press play and tell her I'm going to the kitchen. Her eyes are focused on the screen, and I don't think she hears me.

I enter the kitchen and open the fridge. I stare at the milk, thinking about our trip to the school. That meeting was unexpected. What does it mean? I told the principal she wouldn't be coming back until I felt she was safe. Do I believe my own words? Is she not safe?

The doorbell pulls me from my thoughts. I close the fridge and descend half the stairs and stop. Through the glass, I see Nancy. I look down at my watch and know I don't have time for this today, but when she knocks again, I don't have the heart to turn her away and open the door.

"Hi, Nancy."

She's bundled up in a puffy hunter's-orange coat, and her short ginger hair is partially covered by a pair of earmuffs.

"It's freezing," she says as she pushes past me into the house. "Why do we live here?" She takes off her coat and gloves and hangs them on the coatrack but leaves the earmuffs over her ears. She doesn't wait for a response and trudges up the stairs to the living room.

I follow her up, then walk past her as she stops at the top of the stairs, unsure where to go. I tell her to join me in the kitchen, and she follows me in. She sits at the counter while I go around to the sink and begin washing dishes.

"Were you there?" she asks as I turn on the water.

I look away from the bowl in my hand. "Last night?"

She gives me a "well, duh" look.

"Yes."

"Was it like they said on TV? Where was Nicole? Did he really stab him during the play?"

I look down at the sink and dunk my hands in the hot water, watching as it glides along the rim of the bowl and crosses over my hands. I reach up to the faucet handle and adjust the temperature. "What are they saying on TV?"

She puts her hands flat on the counter, leaning forward on the stool. "They said Shawn, the boy who stabbed the other kid, brought a real sword and used it. They interviewed one parent who said Shawn is always angry. I guess the parents of the boy who was killed are going to sue the school. The teacher and principal are going to get fired."

"Hmm," I say, pulling a dish towel from below the sink and drying the bowl.

"Do you think they will?"

I shrug.

Nancy's face clouds with concern. "How's Nicole? Is she okay? Where was she? Was she in danger?"

I hear Nicole laugh from her room. She must have reached the part where Vizzini, the leader of the gang, is talking with the giant and swordsman on the boat. Vizzini repeatedly utters the term "inconceivable," and Nicole laughs every time he does. My favorite is when she repeats it with him, saying "inconceidable" instead of "inconceivable."

"She's fine. She wasn't hurt."

"Oh, thank God for that. If you ask me, that father bears some responsibility."

I think about my mother and leave the sink, heading back to the fridge.

"The father?"

"Don't you think?"

"Whose father?" I ask as I pull eggs from the fridge and place them on the counter while reaching for a frying pan. Mother loves eggs. If there's one thing I can get her to eat, it's scrambled eggs with a piece of toast.

"The killer. His father had to know his kid was bringing a real sword." She drops her voice to a conspiratorial whisper and leans over the counter. "You know he has no mother?"

I mix the eggs in a bowl and look at her. "No?"

She shakes her head. "Divorced. They say she left him for a younger man. They were nearly forty when they had Shawn. Only child."

Hmm, I think. *Sounds familiar.* I mix in salt, pepper, and onion powder, then put the frying pan on the stove and turn on the heat.

"It's such a shame when a child grows up without a mother. They never turn out right. Even when they're..." She lets the rest of her statement go unsaid when she sees my eyes on her. "Anyway, do you have school tonight?"

I pour the eggs from the bowl into the frying pan. "Yep."

"How late will you be out?"

"Nine."

My back is to her while I stir the eggs. For the first time since she came in, she's quiet. I turn around to see what has her attention. She's looking out the sliding glass door that exits to our deck and backyard. I pull the toaster from the cabinet below the counter and plug it in, then go to the pantry and bring out a loaf of bread.

Her attention remains on something in the backyard, and I walk to the sink and look out the window. My neighbor behind me is chopping wood.

"Do you know him?" she says when she sees me looking out the window.

I step away from the sink and move back to the stove, stirring the eggs, then putting a piece of bread into the toaster and pulling down on the lever. "Who? Ed?"

She's chewing on her fingernail as she stares at him. "He's kinda cute."

I turn back to the eggs and turn off the heat. I get down a plate and pour half onto it. "So is Jake," I say, winking at her.

She looks away from the window and sees me smiling.

"I'm just saying. Have you talked to him? What's his last name?"

"Warner," I say when the toast pops up. I get a knife, butter it, and place it on the plate beside the eggs.

"So, you have talked to him?" She smiles. "Is there something going on?"

I scoff. Since my husband died, I haven't thought about another man. My interactions with Ed Warner have been brief, but I've learned enough to know that even if I did find him attractive, I could never be interested. "No, definitely not." I put a fork on the plate, then look at her. "Listen, I've got to take this down to my mother, then get something for Nicole before I leave for school."

She takes one last longing look at Ed, then nods and walks with me to the stairs. When we reach the landing, she turns back to me while putting on her coat. "How is she?"

"Declining," I say, looking down.

She puts on her gloves and reaches for me. We embrace, and she opens the door.

"How much longer does she have?"

I look away. "The doctors say only a month."

She looks at me with concern. "What are you going to do?"

"I don't know. I'll figure it out."

I shut the door and continue to my mother's room. When I reach it, I see Mom is still in bed, not bothering to dress for the day. I pull a TV tray over and put the eggs and toast before her. She looks down, picks up the fork, and puts some eggs into her mouth.

"You have school tonight?"

I nod.

"Have you talked to her about last night?"

I shake my head and lean against the wall.

Mom takes a bite of her toast and chews, then swallows. "Why not?"

"You know why."

Mom pauses *Matlock* and frowns at me. "You need to talk to her, Sherry."

I shake my head. "Mom, she's fine. She'll get over it. Just like she did with her dad."

Mom picks up her fork. "How do you know she's over that?"

I frown. "She stopped coloring in black."

"So?"

"Mom..."

Mom puts down her fork and looks me in the eye. "Sherry, stop making assumptions. Talk to her. Something isn't right."

Chapter 10
Hank

When we walk into the jail, Officer Levy sees us and nearly runs as she approaches.

"Boy, am I glad to see you."

"What is it, Carol?" Joyce asks.

"You know Shawn Luelan, the boy from the school last night?"

"Yes."

"Well, his father and his lawyer were just here. They were demanding we let him go, but Captain Rigby won't have it. He says he killed a person and can't be set free until we understand more about it. The lawyer said that was against the law unless he's charged with a crime. That's when Captain Rigby said he *is* being charged with a crime—murder. The lawyer left, and I think he's going to talk to the judge. Did you know about this?"

Joyce shakes her head.

"What judge?" I ask.

"Judge Ramsey. He's supposed to be arraigned in a few hours."

Officer Levy clenches and unclenches her fists.

"So, what's going on now?" Joyce asks.

Officer Levy turns and looks back down the hall. "It's the boy. He won't calm down. We had to restrain him. He won't stop screaming."

"Take us to him," Joyce says.

We walk with her down the hall until we reach a cell. There's no need for her to tell us when we reach him. We've heard him screaming all the way down the row of bars.

Shawn lies on his chest on the bed. His arms are restrained behind his back, and his legs are bound at the ankles. He cries for several seconds, then resumes screaming.

"Shawn?" Joyce calls.

He doesn't look at her and begins thrashing on the bed.

"Shawn," Joyce calls to him again. "I hear you like Elvis Presley. Is that right?"

The kicking stops and Shawn groans.

"I like Elvis too. My favorite is 'Suspicious Minds.' Do you know that one?"

Shawn stops and turns toward her. Tears and snot cover his face. "'Hound Dog,'" he mumbles with his chin resting on the mattress.

"'Hound Dog' is your favorite?"

"Uh-huh."

"Do you want to listen to 'Hound Dog'?" Joyce asks, holding out her phone.

Shawn nods, glancing at me, then back to her.

Joyce presses several buttons on her phone as Officer Levy and I watch. The voice of Elvis erupts from the small speaker.

You ain't nothin' but a hound dog

Cryin' all the time
You ain't nothin' but a hound dog
Cryin' all the time

Shawn turns to the side, a large smile spreading across his face. The change is remarkable. As the song plays, the boy relaxes more and more. After several seconds, he begins to sway to the music. Officer Levy looks at Joyce, then at me in open-mouthed amazement.

"Carol?" Joyce says in a whisper. "Do you have the keys to his cell?"

She nods.

"What about his restraints?"

Again, she nods.

"Open the cell."

Officer Levy looks at me, then back at Joyce. "Are you sure?"

Joyce nods. "Open it."

Officer Levy steps to the gate and opens it while Shawn continues to dance, lying on his side, unaware that the gate was opened.

"I hope you're right about this," Carol says.

Joyce looks at her and winks. "There are three of us and one of him. And we have a Hank."

We all smile, and Joyce steps into the cell, followed by me. The song ends, and Shawn looks at us curiously.

"Shawn, did you hear what Elvis said in that song? He said only hound dogs can cry all the time. Are you a hound dog?"

Shawn shakes his head.

"Have you been crying all the time?"

His expression changes again.

Joyce cuts him off before he can cry. "Would you mind if we listened to 'Suspicious Minds' next?" Joyce asks.

"I like that one," Shawn says.

Joyce dials it up on her phone, and when the music plays, Shawn goes back to swaying on his bed.

"Do you trust me?" Joyce whispers to me with a twinkle in her eye.

"Sometimes."

She grins and hands me the phone, then takes several steps back to Officer Levy. She asks the officer for the restraint key, then approaches Shawn. She sits beside him on the bed. "Should we take these off of you?" she asks, pointing to the restraints.

Shawn nods.

Joyce unlocks them, then instructs Shawn to sit on the side of the bed with his large legs outstretched.

"Now, isn't that better?" she says, rubbing his shoulder.

He smiles and sways to the music.

When the song ends, Shawn looks at me.

"What do you like?"

I wasn't expecting that question and can't think of an Elvis song for the life of me. I look down at Joyce's phone and scroll through the options. I recognize only one.

"I like 'Jailhouse Rock.'"

He holds up two big fingers. "Second favorite," he says, pointing to himself.

"Is that right?" Joyce says. "Do you want to listen to that next?"

He nods.

"We'll listen to that if you can answer a couple of questions for us. Would that be okay?"

Shawn watches her, then nods.

"Were you in the play last night?"

Shawn nods. "Raul," he says, pointing to himself.

Joyce gazes at him with a look of approval. "I heard you were really good."

"I sword fighted. I practiced with Roy."

"Was Roy the Phantom?"

Shawn smiles and covers half his face with his hand like he's wearing a mask.

Joyce snaps her fingers and smiles. "That's right. He wore a mask on one side of his face. Did anything happen last night different from your practices?"

Shawn looks confused.

"Was last night different with Roy? The Phantom?"

"Lots of people watched." He gets an idea, and his eyes light up. "My dad came and saw me. He says I was really good."

Joyce nods. "What about with Roy? Did anything happen with him?"

"He did it wrong."

"What did he do wrong?"

"He was supposed to run away but he didn't. He laid down. I tried to tell him to run. But he didn't."

Joyce looks over at me, then removes her gun from her holster. She shows it to Shawn.

"Shawn, do you like guns?"

Shawn nods excitedly.

"Have you ever shot one?"

Shawn shakes his head.

"Would you like to?"

Shawn nods again, giggling.

Joyce hands him the gun and ignores the look I'm giving her. He takes it and points it at himself while looking down the barrel. She turns it around and teaches him how to hold it, putting his finger on the trigger.

"Do you want to shoot it?" she asks.

He giggles and nods. Shawn holds the gun with his finger on the trigger and points it at my chest. I begin to move out of the line of fire, but Joyce holds out her hand, telling me to stop. Again, I give her a look, but she ignores it.

"Okay, Shawn. Shoot the gun at Detective Gardner. Pull the trigger."

Without hesitation, Shawn pulls the trigger, and the gun clicks.

Chapter 11

Sherry

At the stop sign, I turn right onto Croft Street. It's late, almost nine thirty, and I'm exhausted. My house is less than a block away. As I focus on the row of houses, I see the light from the streetlamp in front of my home. My eyes droop as I imagine the warmth of my bed.

As I tap the brake pedal, preparing to pull into the driveway, red and blue lights shine in my rearview mirror. I turn and look, seeing a police cruiser behind me. I pull into the driveway without opening the overhead garage door and keep my eyes trained in the mirror. The officer stops at the end of the drive, just behind me. He puts the car in park but leaves the lights on. He opens his car door and comes around my vehicle, flashing his light inside my windows, examining each before reaching me. I roll down my window and take a quick, short breath as the bite of the air reaches me.

"Good evening, ma'am," he says, eyeing me.

"Hello."

He looks around my vehicle, then at the house. "Is this your home?"

"Yes."

He nods. "I bet you're anxious to get inside. Cold night."

I don't respond.

After a beat, he says, "Long day?"

"Yes."

He nods and leans forward. "Do you know why I've pulled you over?"

I've got a pretty good idea, but why should I tell him?

"No."

He frowns. "Are you from around here?"

"Um, yes."

"Just thought maybe you were from California with that stop back there," he says, shrugging.

Does he think I'm going to laugh at this? I fight back the retort and sit patiently, waiting.

He watches me.

"Are you saying I didn't stop?"

"Did you?" he says, his breath visible in the light from my house.

"I thought I did," I say, trying to control my frustration. Does this guy really have nothing better to do than harass women at nine thirty at night on a weekday as they roll through a stop sign near their house on a deserted street?

He shakes his head.

"Okay, then I didn't," I say, more clipped than I intend.

He examines me, a line appearing on his forehead.

"I'm sorry," I say, exhaling. "I'm really tired. I just came from night school. It's been a really long day, and I still have things to do before I can sleep. I normally stop completely."

He nods and looks away from me at the house.

"I appreciate you reminding me, sir."

His eyes find mine. "Just stop completely, even when you're tired. All right?"

"I will. I promise."

He steps back. "Enjoy your evening. Get some rest."

I smile. "Thank you, Officer."

He walks back to his car, and I roll up the window before opening my garage. He pulls away, and I enter the garage and shut it behind me. I sit in the darkness, willing myself to move. After several minutes, I open the car door.

When I walk into the house, I hear the TV down the hall in my mother's room. As I grow closer, I see Nicole is sitting on the bed beside her. Her grandmother is propped up with pillows, her glasses on, but her eyes are closed. Nicole glances at me as I enter the room, but her focus remains on the TV. She's clenching her hands in her lap.

"You're still up?" I say, going to her and kissing the top of her head. I look at my mother. She still hasn't stirred.

Nicole doesn't respond. Her eyes are troubled as she watches the screen.

I turn and see a man in a light trench coat and tie talking to another man. He holds a cigar between his fingers and rests his thumb on his forehead. He seems confused by something the other person said. I recognize the show, hurry to the remote, and turn off the TV. My mother stirs as I lean across the bed.

"Sherry?" she mumbles, not opening her eyes.

"Yes, Mom," I say. I reach for Nicole's hand. "Come on, honey. Let's get you to bed."

She stands and walks with me toward the door.

"I must have dozed off," Mother says from behind me.

I shake my head in frustration as I guide Nicole down the hall to the stairs. How could she let her watch something like that after what she just witnessed? I know she's old and sick, but she should know better. That man on the screen was investigating a murder. A murder Nicole likely watched.

When we reach the top of the stairs, I have Nicole use the bathroom and brush her teeth while I get out a set of pajamas and place them on her bed. She enters the room, and I help her dress, asking her about her night. She answers in one-word sentences, telling me it was "fine" and she did "nothing."

I pull back the covers and help her into bed. I lean down to kiss her cheek. When I tell her "Good night," she grasps my hand.

"Mama?"

"Yes, honey?" I say, bent over, looking into her gray eyes.

"Why do people hurt?"

I sit down beside her. My lips compress as I consider how I might answer her question. I don't quite know how she means "hurt" and decide to take the more likely scenario.

"Sweetie, sometimes people get old. Your grandma has lived a long, full life. Now her body is tired."

She frowns.

"Don't worry. You're young. You still have many years before that happens to you."

I can see she's troubled, and my answer didn't help. I watch her trying to think of something else to say and decide to address the other option. "Did someone hurt someone else on the TV?"

Her eyes widen and she nods.

"Did that scare you?"

She nods again.

I exhale and look at the pillow beside her. "Honey, that was just pretend. Nobody got hurt. They were just acting. Like you did when you played Christine in *The Phantom of the Opera* play. Remember? You were still Nicole. Shawn wasn't really Raul. Roy..."

I stop myself and look at her. I'm not helping anything. I need something to distract her, or she'll be in the throes of a seizure.

"Did Marilyn call you today?"

Her eyes leave the ceiling and focus back on me. She nods.

"Did she miss you at school?"

She nods again. "She's my friend."

I smile. "Did you miss your friends today?"

She nods. "Can I go tomorrow?"

"To school?"

Her head bobs.

I smile and put my hand on her cheek. "Let's see how things are in the morning."

I turn out her light and close her door. I want so badly to cross the hall and retire to my room, but I know I can't. I descend the stairs and reenter my mother's room. She's awake and has the TV back on. It's still tuned to the same program.

"Mom," I say, looking down at her, hands on my hips.

She looks up at me. She can see my frustration.

"I know. I'm sorry. I was watching Tim the toolman and fell asleep. She wanted to watch it with me."

I sit down beside her. "*Home Improvement*, Mom? It's called *Home Improvement*." I look back at the TV as Columbo interrogates the murderer by asking, "Just one more thing."

She points the remote at the TV and pauses the show. "How was she?" she asks.

I stand from the bed and cross the room, pouring a cup of water and palming several pills, then handing them to her. She takes them from me, and I give her the cup of water.

"She saw the murder on TV. She didn't understand it. You've got to be more careful about what will come on the screen if you fall asleep."

She puts the pills in her mouth and the cup to her lips. She swallows, then gives me back the cup. I put it on her dresser and turn out the lights. She goes back to watching Columbo, and I exit the room. As I climb the stairs, I wonder how long she was asleep tonight. How long Nicole was alone. What did she do during that time?

I enter my bedroom and go to the bathroom. I turn on the light and stare at my reflection in the mirror. How much longer does Mom have? The doctor said maybe a month. Next, my thoughts go to Nicole. I know I need to talk to her. But I'm frightened. I can't forget what happened when I talked to her about Ron. I don't want to put her through that again.

Chapter 12
Hank

"Hank, Joyce, sit down."

The captain motions to the seats opposite him. I've never liked the chairs in his office. They're too much. They have too much cushion, which shrinks the amount of space between the armrests. That's not good for someone like me. I look over at Joyce with envy. She's occupying only half the seat, looking very comfortable.

"Thanks for seeing us, Captain," Joyce says.

He nods and looks at his watch. He's across the desk in his swivel chair with the large back and plenty of room.

"I don't have a lot of time. What did you want to talk about?"

She crosses her legs. "You need to withdraw the charges from Shawn Luelan and let him go home."

Captain Rigby points to his chest. "I *need* to withdraw the charges? Am I the district attorney and nobody told me?"

"You know what I mean. Don't play coy. You know very well your influence."

He lets out a soft, sarcastic chuckle. "I'm flattered, Detective Powers, that you think so much of me." He picks up a pen and turns to the side of the desk, putting it to his mouth and leaning back. "Do I need to remind you that this boy killed one of his classmates while all of them, their teachers, and their parents watched? Not to mention the school administrators."

"It was an accident," Joyce says. "He didn't know what he was doing?"

Captain Rigby looks up at the ceiling. "No?"

"No."

"How do you know that?"

"Because we've talked to him. We've talked to the principal and his teacher. He didn't mean to do it."

He turns back to her. "They said that?"

"Not exactly."

He shrugs and chuckles again. "So, what? This is just another one of your 'gut feelings'? Something you just 'know'?" He sits up in his chair and swivels back to face us. "Detective, I'm not saying you aren't right. Your record speaks for itself. You see things others don't. But," he raises an index finger, "that won't convince the district attorney."

"Dale," Joyce says, her voice hard, "stop being a bureaucrat and start being a person."

Captain Rigby glares at her, and I can see his anger rise.

"Sir," I interject. I glance at Joyce and back at him, shaking my head and holding up a hand. "She didn't mean that."

"Yes, I did," Joyce says, looking away.

"No, you didn't," I tell her, looking back at the captain. "We just came from seeing Shawn. Joyce tested him."

"What do you mean?"

"She gave him her gun and told him he could shoot me."

Captain Rigby's eyebrows go up. "What?"

"It wasn't loaded. He aimed it right at me and pulled the trigger."

"See," Captain Rigby says, raising his hand. "We're dealing with a killer."

I glance at Joyce. She turns back, watching me. I shake my head. "No, that's just it. He didn't know what he was doing. He didn't understand that it would kill me. He's too innocent."

"He's eighteen years old and almost as big as you. He knew what he was doing."

"No, he didn't," Joyce says.

He puts his hands on the desk and looks at us. "So what? He's still dangerous."

"Only if he has a weapon," I say.

Captain Rigby shakes his head. "Let's just assume for a second that he didn't know what he was doing, that he didn't intentionally kill that other boy. What then? Someone put him up to it? Someone told him to do it?"

"No," Joyce says. "Someone put a real sword on the stage, knowing he wouldn't feel the difference. And even if he did, he wouldn't understand the implications."

Captain Rigby looks from me to her. "Who?"

"We don't know yet," I say.

He sinks back into his chair and exhales. "It doesn't make sense. Why would anyone want to kill the other kid? He was in the special class too, right?"

"Yes, but according to his teacher, he was the highest functioning of the kids in the class. He understood more than the others."

"He witnessed something?"

"Maybe," I say.

He swivels to the side again and looks up at the ceiling. After several seconds, he turns back. "If you find out what he knew, or who might have been behind it, I'll see what I can do to get the charges dropped."

I nod and stand to leave. Joyce joins me, but Captain Rigby stops her.

"Joyce, I've warned you before, and I won't do it again. I'm the captain, not you. This is my office, not yours. I won't hesitate to discipline you if I must."

Chapter 13

Hank

After leaving Captain Rigby's office, Joyce tells me she'll meet me in the car and heads down the hallway in the opposite direction. I stop by my desk to look up Roy Edwards's home address, then go out to the car and punch it into the GPS. After several minutes, Joyce exits the building and gets in the car.

"Where'd you go?" I ask, pulling out of the parking space.

"How's your stomach?" she says, not looking at me.

"Fine."

She nods, looking out the window.

"Maybe a Coke would settle your stomach. I think you still owe me from the last one."

She looks over and I grin. She turns up the radio and watches me. "Double or nothing?"

I shake my head, turning the steering wheel.

"Why not?"

"I don't need another Coke."

"You don't know the song."

"Are you sure about that?"

"Positive."

I look away from her and focus on the road. At first, I think she's right. Then the song reaches its chorus.

And you shook me all night long

Yeah, you shook me all night long

And knocked me out, I said you shook me all night long

You had me shaking and you shook me all night long

Yeah, you shook me

Well, you took me

I smile and keep my eyes on the road. "'You Shook Me All Night Long.'"

She snorts. "Yeah, but by who?"

I grip the steering wheel and make a pained expression. "For some reason, electricity feels like it's running through my body." I turn to her. "Do you feel it?"

Her eyes narrow.

"AC/DC, baby."

She gives me a disgusted look, and I throw back my head and laugh.

"How'd you know that?"

I pull into the Maverik and park next to the store. I exit the car and enter. We get our drinks and she pays, glaring the whole time. When we're back in the car, she sips from her straw.

"What's with you and Rigby?" I ask.

She gives me a look, then turns back to the window. "I've known him a long time."

"Yeah...I know."

She grits her teeth. "Have you ever known anyone who changed from who they were? Maybe made a bunch of money or something and became someone else?"

I nod. "A guy I played football with at Boise State. He made it to the NFL and won Rookie of the Year. He and I were super tight in college, and now I don't even talk to him. He doesn't return my texts."

She turns away from the window. "Who?"

I frown at her. "This isn't about me. This is about you and Rigby."

"You never told me how you knew it was AC/DC."

I shake my head and pull into the neighborhood, seeing that we're only three minutes away from the house.

"You've been practicing," she says. "What do you do? Go home each night and study rock songs?"

I smile and keep my eyes on the road. She doesn't need to know there's a song game you can play on Alexa. And she definitely doesn't need to know there's hardly a night Sandra and I don't play it.

I pull the car to the curb, put it in park, and shut it off. "Rigby," I say, looking at her. "You think he's changed?"

"Don't you?"

"I haven't known him as long as you have."

"Still, I know you can see it. When I first knew him, maybe twenty years ago, he was a junior detective. A few years younger than you are now. That man would have fought for Shawn. He wouldn't have allowed him to stay in jail. I meant what I said. He's becoming a bureaucrat."

"He didn't like you saying that."

She snorts. "What's he going to do? I'm retiring in six months."

I shrug and grip the handle, but she reaches over and grabs my arm.

"Promise me you won't change like him."

"I'm not the captain."

"Not yet."

Our eyes lock, and I open the door and get out.

We walk up the drive to the front door. The steps are icy, and I offer Joyce my hand as we climb them. When we reach the front door, I knock and step back. They've got a camera doorbell, and Joyce waves, assuming someone is watching us.

"Yes?" someone says through the speaker.

Joyce pulls out her badge and shows it to the camera. "My name is Joyce Powers. We're detectives with the Idaho Falls Police Department."

"What do you want?"

"Are you Mrs. Edwards?"

"Yes."

"We'd like to speak with you for a few minutes."

"About Roy?"

"Yes."

There's a prolonged silence.

"Give me a few minutes."

Joyce looks up at me, then turns and looks around the neighborhood. "This is pretty close to your house, isn't it?"

"It is."

We look at the houses across the street. It's a chilly day, but the sun is out, and with it shining, it's bearable.

"Who was the player?" Joyce asks.

I smile. "I thought you were a detective. Figure it out yourself. By the way, how's your stomach?"

We hear footsteps behind the door and turn back.

"Better," she says as the door opens.

A woman with artificially tanned skin stands before us. The lines on her face are pronounced, making her seem older than she probably is. Her hair is mostly blond with dark roots visible.

"You can come in," she says, stepping behind the door.

We enter as she kicks the kids' coats and boots out of the way.

"We'll go in the kitchen," she says, leading us to the back of the house.

She's wearing black leggings and an oversized, red sweatshirt with the University of Utah written on the front. She has on wool socks. As we follow her toward the back of the house, I notice the bare walls, aside from the smudges and holes in the drywall. We sit at the kitchen table with mismatched chairs.

"Can I get you anything?" she says as we sit.

"We're fine," I tell her. "Are you from Utah?"

"Grew up there," she says as she sits, and I notice behind her are several bowls with spoons and a cereal box with a carton of milk on the counter. She looks over at Joyce, but seeing Joyce surveying the room, she looks back at me. "I hope that boy is in jail," she says.

"Which boy?" I ask.

"The one who killed Roy," she says with disgust.

"Can you tell us about Roy?"

"What do you want to know?"

"Anything you can tell us?"

Joyce focuses her eyes back on the woman.

"He wasn't my kid. I'm not actually his mother."

"No?"

She shakes her head. "He's my husband's. Had him with his first wife."

"Oh?"

"Yeah, but don't bother trying to find her. She split. Ran off to Rock Springs or somewhere. Likes having money stuffed in her panties. Roy's been with us since."

"Hmm. How long has Roy been living with you?"

"Maybe ten years."

"Long time," I say.

She looks at Joyce, but Joyce says nothing, leaving me to ask the questions.

"It looks like you've got a few kids here in the house besides Roy," I say.

She scoffs. "You could say that."

"How many?"

"Six. Well, five now. Four of my own. Roy has a sister." She shrugs. "April's gone now anyways. She moved out with her boyfriend."

"How old is she?"

"Nineteen. Just a year older than Roy."

"Is your husband home?"

She shakes her head. "He's out in Wyoming. He drives truck. Won't be home until tomorrow."

I nod. "I understand Roy was pretty high-functioning. He was in the special class but pretty capable?"

She shrugs. "If you say so."

"You don't think so?" Joyce asks.

She scowls. "It's not polite for me to say what I think."

Joyce and I look at each other.

"Did you know Shawn? The boy he fought with on the stage?" I ask.

"The big one? The one who killed him?"

"Yes."

She exhales. "Not really. I saw him at the school once or twice. Heard Roy talk about him."

"What did Roy say about him?"

She tilts her head. "They were friends, I guess. That's why I can't believe the kid killed him. And where were the teachers? How did the sword get onstage? We've got a good mind to sue the school." She shifts her focus to Joyce. "Do you know any good lawyers?"

"No," Joyce says. "Do you know anyone who would have wanted to hurt Roy?"

She laughs. "Roy? Nobody wanted to hurt Roy. Why would they? He wasn't a threat to anyone. Scrawny kid. He was annoying, though." She tilts her head. "You think someone wanted the big kid to hurt him?"

"We didn't say that," Joyce says. "What about someone at school? Was there anyone he mentioned? Anything unusual?"

She puts a finger to her chin and looks up. "No. Well, a couple days ago he said something about one of the girls in his class." She chuckles. "Maybe it was his teacher. He could be so annoying with all the questions."

I can see Joyce is losing patience and I jump in. "Which girl?"

"Huh?"

"You said he said something about a girl in his class."

"Oh, right." She bites her cheek. "The short one. Mindy, maybe?"

"Mindy? Not Nicole?"

She snaps her fingers. "Nicole. That's it."

Joyce and I both sit forward.

"What did he say about her?" Joyce asks.

"Something about her having a secret." She shakes her head. "But that isn't anything new. Roy thought someone having a favorite color was a secret. He always said things about secrets."

Joyce and I look at each other, then Joyce returns her focus to Mrs. Edwards. "Did Roy have a bedroom?"

She nods. "He shared a room with my son Eddie."

"Can we see it?"

"It's a mess."

"That's okay."

She guides us down the hall to the staircase that leads to the basement. We dodge piles of clothes and kids' toys all along the way. The bedroom is small and sparsely furnished. There's a bunk bed against the wall and two small dresser drawers with a closet. One of the dresser drawers is white, and the other is the color of unfinished wood. One dresser has a picture of a monster truck hanging above it, while the other has a picture of a Broadway play.

"Roy's?" Joyce asks, pointing to the dresser.

Mrs. Edwards nods.

"Do you mind if I take a look inside?"

She grunts. "Take anything you want. Saves me from getting rid of it."

Joyce stares at her for a moment, then says, "I don't think we'll take anything. We just want to look inside." Joyce opens the top drawer, then points to the bed. "Which bunk was Roy's?"

"The bottom."

I step to it and look around. I drop to a knee and look under it but find nothing other than some crumpled clothes. When I stand, I notice Joyce holding a framed picture.

"Do you know what this is for?" Joyce asks, showing the picture to Mrs. Edwards.

She steps forward and squints at it. "Roy got some kind of award from the school. He always had it out on the dresser."

"On top?" Joyce asks, shutting the drawer from where she had pulled the picture.

"Yeah."

"You don't know what it was for?"

She shakes her head.

I lean over her shoulder so I can get a look at the picture. It's Roy shaking hands with Principal Skinner. His other hand holds a trophy. Several other faculty members, including Ms. Thomas, watch and clap.

"Can we have this?" Joyce asks.

She nods.

After looking around a bit more, we tell Mrs. Edwards we're ready to go, and she walks us back upstairs. When we reach the door, Joyce turns back to her as she follows behind.

"Ma'am, have you ever been to Japan?"

"What?"

"Japan. Have you ever been there?"

"I've never been out of the country."

"What about anyone else in the family? What about your husband?"

She shakes her head. "Why are you asking such strange questions? He died at the school. Everyone saw it. What are you looking for?"

Joyce looks past her as if she hadn't heard. After several seconds, she nods and opens the door and steps out. Mrs. Edwards looks up at me for an explanation.

"Thank you for your time today. We really appreciate it."

Chapter 14
Sherry

I open the garage door and groan. I hadn't looked out the window or checked the weather report, and now I see it snowed. Again! Nicole stands beside me, and I ask her to get in the car. Then, I grab the shovel and start running tire stripes in the driveway. When they're at least two widths wide, I lean the shovel against the wall and get in the car. I don't have time to do the whole thing. At least I did this much. I pull out, making sure my tires don't stray from the visible lines of concrete.

At the stop sign, I glance back at Nicole. She holds her red backpack in her lap. She's wearing black boots and red gloves. She looks so cute. She sees me watching her and smiles. I turn back to the road. This was the right decision. She needs this.

"Are you excited to see your friends today?"

"Uh-huh."

This morning, after she woke, she asked if she could go back to school. I hesitated, but if she saw it, she gave no sign. Earlier in the morning, I made a promise to myself. If she asked to go back, I would let her.

I pull the car into the school parking lot, my tires crunching against the piled snow and salt on the roads. I find a spot in one of the "guest" spaces and come around the car to help Nicole out of the vehicle. Her gloved hand holds mine as we walk together through the lot and along the sidewalk. We enter the school and check into the office. Class has already begun, and I tell the secretary I will take her to her classroom.

When we reach her homeroom, I see Ms. Ferguson is up at the whiteboard. She's teaching simple addition, and the two kids in the class are only vaguely paying attention. Three of the desks are empty. One desk has decorations covering it. It must be Roy's. Balloons and cards cover every inch.

After only a few seconds, Ms. Ferguson sees us and motions to Georgette Thomas, who's sitting beside Marilyn. Georgette stands and walks over as Marilyn and Ty turn to see where she's going.

"Yes! Nicole! You're back," Ty exclaims and begins playing pencil drums on his desk while adding percussion sounds with his voice.

"Hi, Nicole," Marilyn says.

Ms. Ferguson smiles but Georgette doesn't. She looks sternly at me, then at Nicole.

"Nicole, you're late. Let's get your coat off and get you to your seat."

She takes her backpack while I help Nicole with her coat and gloves. Georgette guides her to her seat. I stay at the back, and after Nicole is settled, Georgette returns to me. I motion with my head, and we got out into the hallway.

"Ms. Thomas, I have a request."

"She's late."

What is it with this woman?

"I know. I'm sorry about that. It's my fault."

Ms. Thomas puts her hands on her hips. "No, Nicole needs to get to class on time. She's responsible."

I stare at her open-mouthed. I can't believe the way she talks to me.

"What's the request?" she asks.

"Can you take special care of her today? She's been through a lot this week, and I worry about her coming back to class so soon."

She compresses her lips while nodding thoughtfully. "Mrs. Morgan, we give each of our students specialized attention every day. As I told you back in the office, the safety of our students is our utmost priority."

I know Ms. Thomas has a lot on her plate, so I don't say what comes to mind first. "I know, but she's especially fragile right now. I'd appreciate you taking it easy on her."

Georgette frowns. "Mrs. Morgan, can I be honest with you?"

I nod only because I feel I have no other choice.

"I've noticed you babying Nicole. Have you ever considered that you might be doing more harm than good?"

That's it. I've had it with this woman believing she knows what's best for my child. I can feel my cheeks burning, and my voice is no longer calm. "Ms. Thomas, have you forgotten what happened here just a few days ago? On *your* watch."

Fire flashes in her eyes, and I can see she wants to lash out, but to her credit, she doesn't. We stare at each other for several seconds, then she takes a slow, deep breath.

"Mrs. Morgan, I can assure you, Nicole is safe with us. We'll look after her."

She doesn't wait for a response and reenters the classroom. I watch her go, fuming. I breathe deeply for several seconds before turning away and heading down the hallway. I can't believe she would talk to me like that. Am I making a mistake leaving my daughter with her? Should I remove her from the school? What about her friends? As I pass the office, I get an idea. I enter and talk to the secretary, Mrs. Wallace.

"Hi, it's me again. I wonder if you could help me with something?"

"Sure," she says, her smile sweet and genuine. I'm amazed at how much it does to ease my fears. "How can I help you, hun?"

I get a pained expression. "Do you remember the other day, when my daughter had the seizure here in the office?"

"Of course." She reaches her hand out and covers mine.

"There was a girl here. Do you remember?"

She puts a finger to her chin. "Tall girl?"

"Yes, exactly."

"Mindy."

"Right, Mindy. Do you think it would be okay for me to talk to her? I noticed she was especially kind to my daughter, and I worry about Nicole and wondered if I could ask her to keep an eye on her."

"Oh, for sure. Let me call her down. She's such a sweetheart."

I put my hand to my chest. "Oh, that would be great."

She moves to the computer and checks her records, then inter-coms the class. I thank her, then sit in a chair and wait. After less than five minutes, Mindy walks in, her long, dark hair falling easily across her shoulders and back. She goes to the secretary while I stand.

"You called me?" she asks.

Mrs. Wallace stands and points to me. "Yes, Mrs. Morgan asked if she could talk to you."

Mindy turns around and sees me standing behind her, her eyes wide with surprise.

"I'm Nicole's mom. Do you remember me?" I extend my hand, and she takes it, smiling. "I saw how sweet you were with her the other day and wondered if I could ask for your help."

She nods with excitement. "Of course."

I motion for her to follow me, and we leave the office. Before I close the door, I thank Mrs. Wallace and wave. Once out in the foyer, I point to a bench and she joins me.

"Like I said, I really appreciate how kind you were to my daugh-ter."

"Oh, I'm happy to. I just love Nicole. She's so cute." Her eyes go wide. "Is she okay? Did something happen?"

"Oh, no, she's fine. But I'm a little worried about her. She was on the stage in the play the other night."

"Oh, right. How awful."

"It was. It terrified her. That's why I wanted to talk to you." She looks at me, confused. "I was wondering if you could keep an eye on her. Make sure she's safe?"

"Oh, for sure. That's my job."

"Your job?"

"Yeah, I'm her peer support. I go to lunch with her. I make sure she's doing good. I watch out for her."

"You do?"

She nods happily.

"Oh, you don't know what a weight that is off my mind. I feel so much better."

She puts a hand on my knee. "I love your daughter. She's so sweet. I'll be extra watchful. You don't have to worry. I'd never let anything bad happen to her."

Chapter 15
Hank

We walk out of Roy's stepmother's home and climb back into the car. I start the engine, holding my hands in front of the vents, knowing the air will be cold but hoping to be wrong. We were in the house long enough for the engine to cool. Rather than put the car in drive, I look at Joyce.

"What do you think?"

She's staring at the home, fingers held to her lips. I can see she hasn't heard me. Rather than distract her, I look at the road.

After what has to be more than a minute, Joyce looks at me. "What?"

I chuckle. "I asked you what you thought. I think you were still in it."

Joyce nods, but again, I see she hasn't heard me. Her eyes stray back to the house. After several seconds, she looks back at me. "I've done it again."

I nod and put the car in drive. Maybe getting distance between us and the home will allow her to focus.

"Sorry," she says as I navigate through the neighborhood. "One more time."

"What's got you so preoccupied? It's been a while since I've seen you like this."

Again, she's silent as she stares through the windshield. I consider prompting her but decide to wait. After several blocks, I lose patience.

"Joyce," I say firmly.

She looks at me.

"What are you thinking about?"

"Two things."

"Good. That's progress. What's the first?"

"The picture."

"Of the award?"

"Yes, the one I found in the sock drawer."

"Okay. Why is that significant?"

She looks back out the window and puts her fingers to her lips again. "I don't know."

I frown and take my eyes off the road. "Then why does it have you so worked up?"

"It was framed."

"So?"

She turns back to me. "Why frame a picture, then put it at the bottom of a sock drawer? Why hide it?"

"I don't know."

"Me neither," she says and shakes her head.

I turn the wheel and consider this for a minute. "What's number two?"

"Do you think there was a secret?"

"I don't know. Do you? Roy's mother didn't seem to put much stock in it. Sounds like Roy had a lot of secrets."

She shakes her head. "Not Roy."

"Nicole?"

She nods. "Do you think it was an accident?"

I eye her, then turn away and watch the road. Finally, I shake my head.

"So, you think someone deliberately put a sword on the stage, knowing Shawn wouldn't know the difference?"

"I do."

"Who?"

I shrug. "Beats me. Do you know?"

She considers for a moment, then turns back to the window. "No. But the answer is in that school."

"A student?"

She shrugs.

"A teacher?"

"Maybe. Or a parent."

We fall silent again, and after several minutes, I pull the car into the school parking lot and cut the engine. We enter through the front doors and stop at the office. Principal Skinner stands at the front desk, talking to the secretary. He sees us enter and gives us a curious look.

"Sir," I say. "Do you have a minute?"

He nods and takes a step toward his office, but we don't follow. He sees and turns back.

"We'd like to spend the rest of the day observing the special education class. Would that be okay with you?"

He looks at the secretary, then back at us. "Sure. Whatever you need. Is there something you've learned? Something we can help with?"

Before I can say no, Joyce says, "We're always open to help. What have you got?"

"What do you mean?"

Joyce shrugs. "You tell us?"

He swallows and looks at the secretary. She's already focused back on her computer.

"I was trying to be helpful."

"So, help," Joyce says. "Did Roy Edwards receive an award from you?"

Principal Skinner frowns. "I don't...maybe."

"You don't remember?"

He shakes his head. I know she has the picture in the car, and I wonder if she brought it with her, but if she did, she doesn't show it to him.

"Do you think one of your students intentionally killed another?" Joyce asks.

The secretary's hands stop moving. She's listening.

"Are you asking me if Shawn wanted to kill Roy?" Skinner says.

"Sure."

He looks past us as a student pushes the door open. The girl looks up at me, then at Joyce, and backs away.

"You can come in, dear," Joyce says and holds the door for her, stepping around her. "Think about it, Mr. Skinner. I look forward to your answer."

Chapter 16

Hank

We walk out of the office and down the hall to the special education room, dodging high schoolers as we go. When we reach the classroom, we find it empty. Curious, we exit the room and watch as more and more students fill the hallway. We overhear conversations and watch as some kids exit the building.

I look at my watch, then back at Joyce. "School isn't over," I tell her.

She shakes her head and motions for me to follow. She walks in front of me, weaving her way through students. Nobody would think Joyce is a high school kid. She could be some of these kids' grandma. She graduated before Kurt Cobain offed himself. But aside from her age, she belongs. She's small, white, and an Idaho native. She doesn't attract much attention.

I, on the other hand, stick out like a crab walking on the sidewalk in Oklahoma. I'm six feet five, two hundred and seventy pounds, black, and from Southern California. I might be closer to these kids in age, but make no mistake, it's me they stare at. Not her.

We reach the end of the hall, and the faint smell has grown to an unmistakable hint of burgers and fries. We step through the entry doors and survey the cafeteria. Within seconds, I see them. They're near the front of the line. Nicole, Ty, and Marilyn stand beside two other girls and a boy. They reach the trays, and one girl systematically hands trays to each kid, then stands at the back of the group as they funnel through selecting their food. I look at Joyce, and we get in line.

The kids get their food and find a table near the center of the room.

"When was the last time you had food in a school cafeteria?" I ask.

"Don't you know you aren't supposed to call women old?" she says without expression.

"I said nothing about being old. You did that yourself."

She glares at me and takes a plate with a burger and fries and puts it on her tray. When we reach the checkout, the lunch lady, who bears a striking resemblance to Chris Farley in the old SNL skits, hairnet and all, stares at us.

"Are you substitutes?" she asks.

"Sure," Joyce says.

The woman looks from her to me, then back. "That'll be two dollars and fifty cents."

Joyce checks her pockets. "Do you take credit cards?"

The woman shakes her head. She looks at me. "Do you have cash?"

I consider telling her no but nod.

Joyce turns back to the woman. "My boyfriend will pay you," she says and walks away.

The woman frowns and looks up at me.

"She's kidding," I say and hand over five dollars. I pick up my tray and find Joyce seated at a deserted table. "Your debt is only growing," I say, sitting at the end of the bench. The seat is too narrow for me to fit normally.

"Did you say something?" Joyce asks, watching the six students at the table in the center.

"Two Cokes and a school lunch," I say, dunking three fries in the ketchup.

"I'm good for it."

I look across the room and see the lunch lady is watching us. "I don't think she's buying your story about being a substitute."

Joyce looks away from the kids. "Maybe she'll call Skinner. Or maybe she thinks I'm a cougar. She's wondering how I did it."

"Did what?" I ask, curious but afraid of the answer.

She smirks. "Pulled such a big, sexy man. I saw her eyeing you."

I laugh, and several kids look over.

A group of students enters the room carrying balloons, stuffed animals, and homemade signs. They move to the front of the room near the stage.

"Hey, can I have everyone's attention?" A boy wearing a school officer's sweater calls out in a loud voice. Surprisingly, the cafeteria quiets, and he turns and motions to the girl standing beside him. She's holding a stuffed teddy bear.

"Hey, everyone. As you guys know, Roy Edwards, one of our students, was killed in a terrible accident a few days ago. He was a senior, and like many of you, I went to school with him since we were little." She pauses and wipes her eyes. "Um," she turns and points to the stage, "this is where it happened." She climbs the steps of the stage and places the teddy bear in the middle. "For the rest of the school year, we're going to leave these items in remembrance of Roy. If you have anything you want to leave, please go ahead. Just make sure it isn't too big."

She motions to the other class officers, and they all bring an item and place it next to the bear. When they're done, they hold hands and turn back to the students in the cafeteria.

"Will you all join us in a moment of silence for Roy?" she says and ducks her head to stare at the floor. The other officers follow suit, then the rest of the student body. After a minute, she raises her head and thanks everyone, and the officers walk out.

We turn our attention back to the special education class. The girl with long, dark hair who handed out the trays stands and tells the other students it's time to go. Everyone follows except Marilyn. She reaches across the table and grabs food from the other plates, putting it on her own like she's a rescuee saved from a deserted island.

The peer-support boy snatches her plate and puts it with his. Marilyn tries to hit him, then lets out a wail and buries her face in her arms as they rest on the table. The boy rolls his eyes and takes his and Ty's trays to the garbage and dumps them while one girl tries to console Marilyn. It doesn't work. The more she tries, the louder

Marilyn gets. The girl waves the group on, and the girl with long, straight, dark hair leads them out of the cafeteria.

"Go with them," Joyce whispers. "I'm staying with Marilyn."

I nod, empty my tray in the garbage, and follow them out.

I keep my distance, observing them as they walk. Ty and the other two students talk about his favorite band, Imagine Dragons, as Nicole walks with them but doesn't take part in the conversation. When they round the corner and are only thirty feet from their classroom, a mischievous smile appears on Nicole's face. She veers away from the group and approaches the group of cowboys we saw bully the Spider-Man kid yesterday. Exaggerating the swing of her arms as she walks, Nicole pulls back her hand and slaps the butt of the closest boy with his back to her. The boy jumps and whips around, looking for his assailant. Nicole stands before him, giggling with her hands on her hips.

"Hey, what the hell?" he says.

She giggles again, calls him "bright eyes," and walks to her homeroom. The girl responsible for her scolds her, then turns to the group of boys and mouths "sorry." All the boys laugh except the one who was smacked. He rubs his backside and shakes his head.

The bell rings, and the halls clear as I enter the classroom. The girl who appears to be the leader sits beside Nicole, and the boy sits beside Ty. Ms. Thomas sees me standing in the back and motions for me to take a seat, so I pull a chair. I watch the class for several minutes before Marilyn stomps into the room. Her peer support rests a hand on her back, trying to console her. Marilyn turns away and slumps at her desk, burying her head in her arms.

"Marilyn," Ms. Thomas says, standing in front of the room. "What's the matter now?"

Marilyn doesn't look up, and the peer-support girl puts her hands up in an "I don't know how to help her" gesture.

"I guess we won't be having that pizza party," Ms. Thomas says.

Marilyn looks up from her desk, and Joyce enters the room beside me. She sits, and we watch the interaction.

"I'm hungry," Marilyn says.

"You just ate lunch," Ms. Thomas says.

Marilyn shakes her head.

"You didn't eat lunch?"

"Not french fries."

Ms. Thomas shakes her head and holds a book in her hand. "It's reading time. Don't you want reading time?"

Marilyn leans back in her chair and folds her arms.

"Don't you?"

"I want french fries."

"You eat enough french fries," Ms. Thomas says, then holds up the book.

For the next hour, we observe the class. When the bell rings and the class aides leave, Joyce whispers, "I'd like to talk to Nicole."

"Can we?" I ask.

"She's eighteen."

"But is she really?"

Joyce stands and walks over to her. Nicole sits alone, coloring in a coloring book.

"Hi, Nicole. My name is Joyce."

Nicole looks at her.

"That's a pretty picture you're coloring. Do you like puppies?"

Nicole nods.

Ms. Thomas sits at her desk watching them, phone in hand.

"That's beautiful."

"I like red," Nicole says.

"I do too," Joyce says, sitting in the seat beside her. "It matches your backpack."

Nicole nods and reaches for it, sitting in the seat beside her. She opens the pouch and pulls out her CDs, showing them to Joyce.

"Would you look at that," Joyce says.

"I like the Oakridge Boys." She reaches into her backpack and pulls out a picture. Four men stand smiling for the photo. Nicole points to each man. "That's Duane. That's Steve. That's Joe. And that's Richard. He has a deep voice." She giggles and gives her best impression, "Oom bop a mow mow."

Joyce laughs. "Is that your favorite song?"

Nicole giggles and nods. She looks through her CDs and opens a case. She puts the CD into the player. While she does it, Principal Skinner enters the classroom, looks at me, then at Joyce. "Detective Powers?"

Joyce turns and looks at him.

"Can I see you outside for a moment?"

Joyce turns back to Nicole. "I'm going to go talk to your principal, then I'll be back. I want to hear that." Joyce drops her voice. "Oom bop a mow mow."

Nicole giggles, and I follow Joyce out the door. Principal Skinner stands in the hall with his hands on his hips. He motions for us to follow him. We walk among the loud and active students until we reach a teacher's lounge. A couple of adults sit on a couch talking, and we move to a corner of the room.

"What were you talking to Nicole about?" Skinner asks.

"The Oakridge Boys."

He frowns. "Nothing about the murder?"

"No."

He eyes her, then looks up at me. "I can't allow you to talk to her about that night."

"You can't *allow* us?" Joyce says, and I can't help but notice the statement sounds an awful lot like the one she said to Captain Rigby about charging Shawn.

He shakes his head. "Her mother is threatening to sue the school. She's only allowed to come if nobody mentions Roy's death. She absolutely forbade it." Skinner looks up at me, then back to Joyce. "Promise me you won't mention anything surrounding Roy's death. Nothing about Shawn."

Joyce nods. "I'll promise...on one condition."

Skinner looks at her warily. "What?"

"You answer my question."

Skinner nods. "What question?"

"Did one of your students intentionally kill another student?"

He frowns. "You know they did?"

"I'm not asking you if one student killed another, I'm asking if it was intentional."

Skinner shrugs. "You tell me."

Joyce's voice becomes hard. "It's a simple question, Principal. You had a murder here a few nights ago. Was it intentional?"

He raises his hands, shocked by the venom in her voice. "I...yes, I guess so."

"Which student?"

"Shawn Luelan. You know that."

"So, you think Shawn intentionally killed Roy? Knew what he was doing?"

Skinner sighs. "I don't know. Maybe?"

"Yes or no?"

Skinner looks at me, then back at Joyce. "No."

Joyce takes a step closer to him. "But you said you 'guess' one of your students intentionally killed Roy. If not Shawn, then who?"

Skinner looks down, rubbing his hand. "I don't know."

Chapter 17
Sherry

I enter the school parking lot and smile. Mindy is standing by the building, talking with Nicole. When I near the curb, Nicole sees me and points to the car. Mindy turns and waves, then helps her over to me, opening the back door and placing Nicole's backpack beside her.

"Thank you, Mindy," I say, turning around in my seat as she stands outside the door.

"You're welcome, Mrs. Morgan."

I wave her to the front, and she shuts Nicole's door, then opens the passenger door.

"How did it go today?"

"Good." She looks back at Nicole. "Right?"

Nicole smiles.

I reach out to Mindy, and she takes my hand. "Thank you so much."

"Happy to help. I'll watch out for her again tomorrow. Don't worry."

She shuts the car door, and I circle the lot, then exit and turn onto Blue Sky Drive. I check the rearview mirror and see Nicole looking out the window on the other side of the car. Because of her height, she can't see out the window beside her.

"Sounds like you had a good day," I say, watching her.

"Yep." She smiles at me.

"Mindy's a sweet girl."

"She's my friend," Nicole says.

"Good to have such a nice friend."

"Uh-huh." Nicole looks back out the window. "People came to the classroom today."

My eyes had returned to the road but flash back to her. "People? What people?"

"Nice people. She likes the Oakridge Boys."

I exhale. "Oh? Well, how could she not? They're the best, right?" She giggles.

We reach our neighborhood, and I see a car parked in front of our house. A big man sits behind the wheel, watching us pull in. A woman with graying hair sits in the passenger seat. When I exit the car and walk around it to help Nicole, I notice they're out of their car and walking down the driveway. I leave Nicole in the car and walk out to meet them. While seated in the car, I could see the man was large. Now, standing beside him, I marvel at his enormous size. I don't get too close. He intimidates me. "Can I help you?"

"Mrs. Morgan?" he says.

"Yes."

"My name is Detective Hank Gardner." He motions to the woman. "This is Detective Joyce Powers." She smiles, and they hold out their badges. "We wondered if we might speak to you for a few minutes."

"What about?"

"Oh, hi," Nicole says from behind me. I turn to see her waving.

"Nikki, do you know them?"

Nicole walks out of the garage with her backpack in her hands. "She's my friend," she says, smiling.

Detective Powers waves at her. "Hi again, Nicole. I didn't get to hear that um-bop-a-mow-mow song."

Nicole giggles and holds up her backpack. "It's in here. Come inside." She reaches for Detective Powers's hand, and Detective Gardner grins at me. Not wanting strangers in the house but unsure how to stop it, I follow as the three of them enter our home. Nicole walks up the stairs, still holding the detective's hand and talking about the house.

"Mom," I call out at the bottom of the stairs. "You okay?"

"Fine," I hear her say from her bedroom. "Who's here?"

"I'll explain later," I say and walk up the stairs behind Detective Gardner. Each step he takes makes the stairs creak.

"How tall are you?" I ask to his back.

When he reaches the middle landing, he turns back and says, "Only six foot five."

"Only?" I say.

He laughs.

Nicole and Detective Powers are at the top of the stairs, and Nicole is pulling her toward the hall, wanting to show off her bedroom.

"Let's ask your mom if it's okay first," Detective Powers says.

"Honey," I say, "I thought you wanted to play 'Elvira' for the nice lady on your CD player? Why don't you do that at the kitchen table? It'll be more comfortable there."

"Okay," Nicole says, guiding Detective Powers to the table. Detective Gardner grins and follows. I motion for them to sit and offer to get them a Coke. Powers makes some comment to Gardner that must be an inside joke and he smiles. I step to the fridge while they sit at the kitchen table with Nicole.

Nicole gets out her music and shows it to Detective Powers. She plays several songs and smiles and giggles as Powers pretends to dance and sway with the music. After fifteen minutes, Detective Powers tells Nicole they have something they want to discuss with me. Nicole is disappointed, but when I suggest she watch *Sesame Street*, she agrees and goes with me to her room. She sits in her chair while I set up the recording on the DVR and shut the door behind me. I go back to the kitchen and join the two detectives, wondering what they want from me.

"Thank you for being so sweet to her," I say to Powers.

"She's so cute. I could stay with her all day."

"Thank you." I look at Detective Gardner. "I have to ask you something."

"Okay?"

"Did you play football at Boise State?"

He chuckles. "I did."

I grin at him. "I knew it. I remember you. It was several years ago."

He nods. "Good memory. I guess you're a football fan?"

"Broncos, baby. I love the Smurf Turf."

He laughs.

"Have you ever seen *The Princess Bride*?" I ask.

He frowns. "I think, maybe. But it was a long time ago."

"There's this guy in it. He's a giant. You kind of remind me of him. But you're much better looking."

He chuckles again. "I'll have to check it out."

I look at Detective Powers. "Is this about the other night?"

She nods.

"I was there, but I don't think I can help you. I saw it just like everyone else."

"What did you see?" Detective Gardner asks.

I look down and trace the grains on the oak table. "The boys were sword fighting. Roy fell, and Shawn helped him up. It was really cute. Nobody knew it was a real sword."

"Didn't you hear it?" Powers asks.

"What?"

"The metal," Powers says.

"No. I mean. The two swords looked a little different, now that I think of it. But at the time, it seemed perfectly normal."

"So, you didn't see anything unusual?"

I shake my head.

"Do you know the other kids in Nicole's class?" Powers asks.

"A little but not well."

"I understand you don't know them well, but do you think Shawn would intentionally hurt Roy?"

"No. No way. Why would he do that?"

Powers looks at me and purses her lips. "Roy's stepmother said Nicole told him she knew a secret."

"She did? What secret?"

Powers doesn't respond, only stares at me. After a few seconds, I find it unnerving and look at Detective Gardner.

"We were hoping you could tell us," he says.

I frown. "I don't know about any secret. She said Nicole? Not Marilyn? You're sure?"

Gardner nods.

"You think it's related?"

Powers shrugs. "We're not sure. It's about the only lead we have right now."

"So you agree with me? You think someone gave Shawn the sword?"

They both nod.

"Well, Nicole hasn't said anything about it to me. If she does, I'll let you know."

Detective Powers watches me. "Would you allow us to talk to her?"

I shake my head. "Look, I appreciate how sweet you are to her, but absolutely not. She doesn't handle things like this well. You saw her smiling with you today? She hasn't been like that since the play. I don't want her to revert back."

"What if we only asked her—"

"No." My eyes smolder in anger. "You have no right to talk to my daughter about anything without my permission. Do you understand me?"

Detective Gardner looks at me with wide eyes, but Detective Powers continues to watch me, unfazed.

"Did you hear what I said?" I say.

Finally, she nods.

I look at my watch. It's time for me to get to class. I stand from the table and tell the detectives. As I walk them to the front door, Detective Powers turns back.

"Mrs. Morgan?"

I don't want to hear what she has to say, but I don't want to be rude either. I'm already feeling a little guilty for how harsh I was earlier. "Yes?"

"Would you ask Nicole?"

I purse my lips. Who is this woman? Doesn't she know how fragile Nicole is? She had a seizure the first time she went back to the school after the tragedy.

"Look, I'm a mother myself. I understand your desire to protect her. But there's a boy sitting in a jail cell right now who needs your help."

Her words about Shawn hit me hard. What if it were Nicole? Wouldn't I be begging for help from others? Even if I think Nicole knows nothing and they're barking up the wrong tree, isn't it my duty to try?

I look her in the eye. "I'm not promising anything, but I'll see what I can do."

Chapter 18
Hank

"Ms. Thomas, can we talk to you?"

Joyce and I had already entered the classroom and found her sitting at her desk, staring at her computer screen.

After leaving Nicole's house, we rushed back to the school, hoping to find her teacher before she left for the day.

When she sees us, she takes off her reading glasses and offers a less-than-pleased look.

"Detectives," she glances at her watch, "I only have a couple minutes before I need to leave, and I've got several emails to respond to."

"Oh, good," Joyce says, walking past me and sitting at a student desk in the front row of the classroom. "We won't be more than a couple minutes."

I bring a chair over and sit down beside Joyce. Ms. Thomas sighs and closes her laptop.

"There's something I've been wanting to ask you," Joyce says.

"Yes?"

"Why did you text Principal Skinner and tell him we were talking to Nicole?"

Ms. Thomas picks up a pencil and examines it. "I didn't."

"Oh?" Joyce says, staring at her.

Ms. Thomas shakes her head.

"Seems like a bad idea to me," I say. Ms. Thomas looks over at me. I put my hand on my chest. "I would never lie to a couple of detectives investigating a murder."

Joyce grimaces and looks back at Ms. Thomas.

"I'm not lying," Thomas says, looking unconvincing.

"Prove it," Joyce says.

"How?"

"Let me see your phone."

Ms. Thomas picks up her phone and hides it below the desk.

"That's what I thought," Joyce says. "So, why then? Why don't you want us talking to Nicole?"

Ms. Thomas watches her, then puts her phone face down on the desk. "She's a kid. You have no right to talk to her without her mother's permission."

"She's eighteen and an adult."

Ms. Thomas makes a face. "Oh, please. She's an innocent child, and you know it."

"An innocent child with a secret," Joyce says.

"What? What secret?"

Neither of us answers, watching her. She fidgets and taps the pencil on the desk.

"I think you know what secret," Joyce says.

Ms. Thomas shakes her head. "I don't. I swear."

Joyce watches her for several seconds, then looks at me, then back at Ms. Thomas. "I'm curious about something. Did you provide the costumes for the play? I assume the kids were wearing costumes?"

Ms. Thomas frowns and looks confused at the change in topic. "The kids' families provided the costumes. They were simple."

"What about the props and the set? How did you do those?"

"Some of the props came from school donations."

"Donations from who?"

She tilts her head. "Parents, other members of the community."

"What about the set? From what I saw, it was pretty elaborate. One part looked like the opera house."

She shrugs. "I can't remember who made it."

Joyce scoffs, and I shake my head, chuckling.

She looks up from the desk. "I can't."

"Sure," I say.

"Now," Joyce says, "I'm even more curious." She looks over to me. "Aren't you?"

I nod. "Seems like she's hiding something."

"Well, if she won't tell us, I bet someone else will."

Ms. Thomas slams her pencil. "Look, his name is Ed, okay?"

"Ed what?" Joyce asks, leaning forward.

"Ed Warner."

"And who is this Ed Warner?" I ask.

She looks at her watch and stands, then puts her laptop in her bag. "He's a local handyman. He heard about the play and wanted to help." She comes around the desk. "I'm sorry, detectives, but I really have to go now."

"Does Ed have a child in the school?" I ask as she walks past me.

We get up and join her in walking to the back of the classroom.

"I don't think he has kids," Ms. Thomas says.

We walk out of the room, and she cuts the lights, then locks the door.

"I really have to go," she says.

"Hot date?" Joyce asks.

Ms. Thomas glares at her and walks away.

"We'll see you tomorrow," Joyce calls to her.

Ms. Thomas rounds the corner, leaving our view. Joyce looks at me and chews on her cheek. "Ed Warner," she says.

I nod. "Strange."

"What's that?"

"He wasn't on the list of people present during the play."

She raises an eyebrow. "Hmm." She walks forward, drumming her fingers on her chin.

"Very curious," I say, falling into step beside her.

For the next ten minutes, we stroll around the halls, looking in open classrooms. Other than an occasional teacher or custodian, we find the school is almost entirely empty.

As we exit the building and walk to our car, we see one other vehicle in the parking lot. It's an old, beat-up 1995 Ford Escort. Between the rust and oxidation, it's hard to tell what color it is. Maybe green, maybe blue, maybe both. As we approach, we see a high school girl sitting behind the wheel. Her head is down, and her beautiful, long, straight, dark hair covers her face. Not wanting to frighten her, but also wanting to make sure she's okay, we approach the car. Likely seeing our shadows, she startles, looking up from her phone. Joyce taps on the window and tells her to roll it down, and after a wary look, the girl complies. With the dirty window no longer obstructing our view, we can see she's been crying.

"What's the matter, young lady?" Joyce asks.

The girl wipes her eyes. "My car won't start."

"Hmm, that won't do," Joyce says.

"Maybe we can help," I say. "What's happening?"

She turns the key and nothing happens. "See? It just started doing this."

"Pop the hood. I'll take a look," I say.

She puts her phone down and opens the door. She gets out and comes around to the front of the car. Her slender fingers fit easily under the hood. She pulls and nothing happens. I smile at Joyce, and she goes to the driver's side and reaches below the steering wheel. She releases the lever. There's a slight pop.

"Try again," I tell the girl.

She pulls, and the hood comes up several inches. She pulls even harder, and I move beside her.

"There's a little lever on the inside," I say, pushing it while gently opening the hood. I locate the prop rod and fit it into place. "Likely your battery."

She looks at the engine and examines the radiator. I nudge her with my elbow and point to the black box on the driver's side. I move the rubber cap from the red positive terminal and see the likely issue.

"You've got a lot of corrosion around those terminals."

Joyce comes around the car and looks, nodding. She walks to our car and pulls a toolbox from the trunk, then comes back and hands it to me.

"Me?" I ask.

"You're the man," she says, smiling at the girl.

"So?"

She winks at the girl. "You know you'd never feel comfortable with us fixing the car. Just get to it."

I sigh and open the toolbox.

"You'll need a wrench for the bolts on the terminals," Joyce says.

"Do you want to do this?"

She looks at the girl. "Why are you here so late?"

"I'm behind in a couple classes."

"You look familiar," Joyce says. "Didn't I see you in the special education classroom?"

I disconnect the black negative terminal.

"Yes. That's sort of why I'm behind."

"Oh?"

"One of the moms asked me to watch out for her daughter. I've been spending extra time with her this week."

"That's very nice of you. Which girl?"

"Nicole."

I get the red terminal disconnected, then find a wire brush and start polishing the terminals, removing all the corrosion I can reach.

"How long have you been helping in the class?"

"All year. Someday I want to be like Ms. Thomas and teach special ed. The kids in the class are so sweet."

"Sad what happened, huh?" Joyce says.

"So sad. I can't believe Shawn would do that."

I glance over at her, then get back to cleaning the terminals.

"Do you think he did it on purpose?" Joyce asks.

The girl shakes her head. "I don't know. He always had a temper. And sometimes Roy would tease him."

I keep an eye on her as I work, putting the terminals back together.

"Really?" Joyce asks. "I hadn't heard that. How would he tease him?"

She tilts her head. "Oh, I don't think Roy meant it. He would just say Elvis sucked. Stuff like that. Shawn loves Elvis."

"Hmm." Joyce holds out her hand. "I'm Joyce, and this is Hank. We're detectives with the Idaho Falls Police Department."

"I know," the girl says. "Everyone knows who you are."

"Really?" Joyce says. "Don't tell me we don't look like high school students."

The girl laughs, and I reconnect the terminals. I walk around to the driver's side and turn the key. The car turns over easily, and the girl squeals with delight, clapping her hands. "Oh, my gosh. Thank you so much."

"My pleasure," I say.

Joyce gives me a look of approval.

"You might want to get that exhaust checked. It's pretty loud," I say.

The girl shakes her head. "Oh, I know. But my mom doesn't want to put any more money into it. And I can't afford it."

"What's your name?" Joyce asks the girl.

"Mindy."

"Mindy," Joyce says. "Make sure you get some grease on those terminals. That'll help them from having so much built-up corrosion."

"How do I do that?"

"Go to an auto-parts store and tell them what happened. They can help."

"I will," Mindy says, sliding into the driver's seat. She closes the door, but the window is still rolled down.

"Can I ask you something?" Mindy says.

"Sure," Joyce and I say in unison.

"Why are you hanging around the school? Everyone knows Shawn killed Roy. We all saw it."

"You were there?" Joyce asks.

She nods.

"We're not convinced Shawn did it on purpose."

She frowns. "What do you mean?"

"We think someone put the real sword there, knowing Shawn would use it."

She looks at me, then back at Joyce. "You mean they wanted Roy to be killed?"

Joyce nods.

"But who would do that?"

"That's what I was going to ask you. Do you know anyone who would want to hurt Roy?"

"You mean other than Shawn?"

Joyce nods.

"No."

"Nicole said Roy knew a secret."

"When did you talk to her?"

"After school."

"And she said Roy knew a secret?"

Joyce nods. "Do you know why Nicole would say that?"

Mindy shrugs. "Nicole has a lot of secrets. She thinks the CDs in her bag are a secret, even though the entire school has seen them." Mindy laughs, and we both smile. "Well, I'd better get home. My mom will be looking for me."

She rolls up the window and drives out of the parking lot as we go back to our car. I put the toolbox in the trunk and get behind the wheel and start the car.

"See, don't you feel better?" Joyce says.

I look at her.

"If I had fixed it, what would it do for your male ego?"

Chapter 19

Sherry

I stand at the bottom of the stairs and call to the top level. "Nicole, you're going to be late. Are you ready?"

I hear footsteps on the floor above me. She's in the bathroom. After several seconds, I hear the water running, and the door opens. She comes down the stairs holding her coat in one hand and her red backpack in the other.

"Do you need help?"

She nods and comes to me. I help her with her coat and gloves, then open the door leading to the garage.

"Will you go get in the car? I want to let your grandma know we're leaving."

"Okay, Mama," Nicole says.

I go down the hall to my mother's room. The door is shut, and I listen with my ear pressed to it. There's not a sound from inside. I slowly open the door and look at my mother lying in the bed. She's silent, and although she rarely snores, I've heard her enough to know she's never soundless. I tentatively walk forward, afraid today will be the day I've dreaded for weeks. Her body lies on the bed, bundled beneath a mountain of blankets.

"Mom?" I say, leaning over her. Panic rises in my chest when she doesn't respond. "Mom," I say more forcefully, bumping her body beneath the blankets.

An eye opens, and she looks at me like she doesn't know me.

"Beverly, are you okay?"

There is a bead of perspiration on her forehead. Her upper lip is glistening. She moans, and her eyes focus. "Sherry?" Her voice is barely more than a whisper.

"I'm here, Mom."

She opens the other eye, focused on me now. "Sherry, something's not right."

I put my hand on her forehead, and I'm shocked by the heat.

"Mom, you're burning up."

She shifts in the bed. "Cold," she croaks.

"You're cold?"

Her nod is so tiny, it's barely perceptible.

"Mom, listen, I've got to get Nicole to school. When I come back, I'll take you to see Dr. Woodbury."

She shakes her head.

"Mom, this is nonnegotiable. You have to see her."

She ignores me.

I look down at my watch. "I'll be back," I say and rush out of the room.

I open the garage and get in the car, looking back at Nicole. Should I keep her home today? If I have to spend the day in the hospital, wouldn't it be easier with Nicole at school?

Nicole watches me with concern. "Is Grandma okay?"

I smile. "She's a little tired. You know how old ladies can get."

I put the car in reverse and exit the garage. It snowed again last night. It's only December, but I'm already sick of this winter. I know I'll regret it, but I don't shovel and drive right over the snow, packing it on the driveway. My tires slip when I reach the street and turn the wheel. More slowly now, I put the car in drive and head down the road. When I reach the stop sign, I turn back and look at Nicole. Her eyes haven't left me.

"Are you okay, honey?"

I look forward again, verifying no other cars are passing, and turn the wheel. I check the rearview mirror and see she's still watching me.

"Are secrets bad?" she asks.

I frown and look back. Her eyes are curious. Is she asking this because of what the detectives said? Does she sense I'm holding back information about her grandma? I was planning to talk to her but wanted to wait until after school.

My eyes return to the road. "Well, honey, that depends. Usually, secrets aren't good. Although, sometimes we don't say things because we know it might hurt someone." I check the rearview mirror, and see she's considering my words. I wish I could read her thoughts. Does she really have a secret? Or is this directed at me? Does she think I'm keeping secrets from her?

We reach the high school, and I pull into the parking lot. I scan the front doors. The school is quiet, not a soul around. I look at the clock on my dashboard and see it's ten minutes after the last bell. All the kids are already in class. I think about my mother and exit the car, debating what to do. I open the door and help Nicole out while considering her question. Should I tell her about her grandmother? Maybe Ms. Thomas was right. Maybe I do baby her.

"Sweetie, I need to get back home to Grandma. She isn't feeling well. Do you think you can go into the school and get to your classroom by yourself? Do you know where it is?"

Her big blue eyes study me and she nods.

I look back at the school and second-guess myself.

Without warning, she leaves my side and walks toward the front doors. I watch her, feeling a surge of pride, and rush back to the car, climbing behind the wheel. She opens the school door and disappears inside without a look back. Impressed, I put the car in drive and pull my phone from my pocket, dialing my mother. The phone rings until a robotic voice tells me the voicemail was never set up. Worried, I end the call and mash the gas, flying through the intersection. I turn east, toward our neighborhood, and lose traction. My car slides and angles toward a parked car on the side of the road. Without thinking, I pull the steering wheel harder, and the car spins out of control. Before I see it, my car slams into the other vehicle.

The impact of the crash whips my head to the side and smashes the window beside me. I shut my eyes and reopen them, dazed and blurry. Moments later, I see the shadow of a man standing just outside the window. He knocks on the glass.

"Are you okay?" he asks.

I struggle to keep my eyes open. "My mother," I say, fighting for clarity. "She needs me."

He pulls on the door as I lose consciousness.

Chapter 20
Hank

"Isn't that his truck?" I say, pointing to the twenty-year-old brown Silverado parked by the curb in front of a two-story house.

Joyce checks the note in her hand, then nods. We exit the car and walk across the street. Fresh snow covers the driveway, and a set of footprints leads to the garage, then stops. We climb the stairs to the front door, and I knock loudly. After a minute, I knock again and ring the doorbell. Again, nobody answers.

"Why isn't he answering? Or the homeowner?" I ask.

Joyce looks around the neighborhood. "Would you?"

I see her point, and she walks down the steps and back to the garage. She circles the garage and opens the gate leading to the backyard. The snow is deep, maybe fifteen inches, and half her leg disappears each time she steps. The depth of the snow affects me less, and I quickly catch and pass her.

There's a walkout basement in the back, and I step to it, knocking. Again, nobody comes. Joyce shrugs and trudges up the stairs to the deck. I follow and see she's already at the sliding glass door when I reach the top. She removes her glove and knocks with her knuckles.

Movement from within the house catches my eye. Joyce steps back as a man approaches the door and slides it open. He wears a baseball cap and has flecks of paint covering his clothes.

"Aren't supposed to be here," he says with a surly tone.

I move over to stand beside Joyce. He takes notice of me and softens the muscles in his face. "Who are you?"

Joyce and I hold out our badges.

"Are you Ed Warner?" I ask.

"Yeah," he mumbles.

"We've been looking for you. You're a hard man to track down."

"Looking for me, why?" He barely opens his mouth when he talks, and everything he says comes out as a mumble.

"Can we come in?"

"Not my house."

"We won't touch anything," Joyce says and pushes past him.

He puffs up his chest, and we step into the kitchen after knocking the snow off our boots. The house is empty. Not a single piece of furniture in sight. The temperature is low, and I wonder if the heat is even on.

Ed leans against the kitchen counter with his arms crossed. "Whatcha want from me? I didn't do nothin'."

"Never said you did," I say.

"Then why you here?"

Joyce steps around him and looks down the hall as he moves away from the counter. "Are you working in this house?"

He shrugs. "It's a big job. I do it myself."

"What, exactly, are you doing? You're a handyman, right?"

"Contractor," he corrects.

"Do you work alone?"

"Had an employee. Couldn't afford him. Damn taxes. How's a man supposed to make any money in this economy? Politicians don't care about guys like me. If it was up to me, I'd put them all on a boat and ship them outta here." His eyes shift back and forth between us. "IRS?"

I chuckle. "No. We're detectives with the Idaho Falls Police Department. Do you know what happened at the school several nights ago?"

He swallows and shakes his head.

"You never heard about the boy who was stabbed on the stage during the play?"

He takes a step back and shakes his head. I can see the muscles in his jaw working.

Joyce looks at him and puts her hands on her hips. "Ed, you're a lousy liar."

His eyes go wide. "Not lying."

She clicks her tongue. "Edward, we know you built the set they used in the play. There's no use in lying to us."

He frowns. "Not lying."

She grins. "Well, excuse me. I didn't realize you've been living under a rock."

"Huh?"

"Idaho Falls is a pretty small town. Would you agree?"

"No."

She frowns. "Oh, come on, Ed. I'm not talking about by Southern Idaho standards. I know Idaho Falls is one of the bigger cities in Idaho. I'm talking about compared to places like New York, LA, Chicago. Would you agree that Idaho Falls is small compared to those cities?"

He shrugs. "I guess."

"And when a kid dies at school, stabbed by a sword, everyone talks about it. It's all over the news. It's all over social media."

"That wasn't my sword," he says defensively.

"What do you mean?" I ask.

He looks up at me. "I made the wooden swords. But that sword wasn't mine. I don't know where he got it."

"So, you do know what happened," Joyce says.

Ed looks at her and takes a step back. "I heard somethin'. But I wasn't there."

"We know," Joyce says. "That surprised us. Why would a man who donated the entire set not attend the performance when it was being used? Why didn't you go, Ed?"

"I don't like plays and stuff and whatever."

"No?" She eyes him with a slight smirk. "Do you know any of the kids in the play?"

He shakes his head.

"None of them?"

Again, he shakes his head.

"You don't know Shawn or Roy or Marilyn or Ty?"

He shakes his head.

"None of those names ring a bell?"

"No."

"What about Nicole?"

His jaw tightens. "Nope."

"She's your neighbor, isn't she? She lives behind you. Your yards touch."

He looks down and shuffles his feet. "The little girl? The short one?"

"Yes."

"I've seen her around. By the house. You know?"

"Have you ever talked to her?"

He shakes his head.

"Hmm," Joyce says. She walks over to the kitchen sink and looks at it. "Ed, have you ever built a set for a stage play before? I saw it. Mighty fine craftsmanship. I'm curious how you have that skill. How did you know how to do that?"

He looks at me, then turns to her. "I worked on them in high school and everything related to it."

"Oh," she says, nodding and looking away from him. "You did a beautiful job." She walks back over to us, standing by the sliding door. "And you made the wooden swords?"

He nods.

"Was that a lot of work?"

"Sorta."

"Do you own any swords, Ed?"

He shakes his head uncertainly.

She looks him in the eye. "Ed, have you ever been to Japan?"

He frowns.

"Did you hear the question?" I ask.

He looks up at me. "Yeah."

Joyce narrows her eyes and holds up her hands. "Yeah, you heard the question? Or, yeah, you've been to Japan?"

"Um, both and everything."

"I thought so," Joyce says. "The way those swords were shaped," she demonstrates the curve of the blade, "I don't know how you did it. They look like swords from Japan. Like the Samurai had."

He nods. "That's how I made them or whatever."

"How did you get the curve in the blade?" I ask.

He looks at me and smiles, chuckling. "There wasn't a curve."

"What? I saw it. The blade curved."

He chuckles and shakes his head. "Nope. It just looks like that. It's the way it's painted."

"Clever," Joyce says. "So, you made the swords and the set?"

He nods.

"Why were you in Japan? Vacation?"

"I went for a mission for my church."

"When you were young?"

He nods.

"Do you own any metal swords?" I ask.

He looks at me, then at Joyce.

"No."

"None that you display or show to people?"

"No."

Joyce looks around the room, then at me. "Thanks for your time today, Ed. Good luck with the rest of the house."

Chapter 21
Sherry

I open my eyes and stare up at the ceiling. The room is bright, but the light is unnatural. There's a beeping noise behind me, and I turn in bed and look for the source. A woman parts the curtain that separates me from other "guests."

"Sorry about that. Did it wake you?" she says, turning off the machine. She leans over the bed and focuses on my eyes. "You look like you're doing better."

My head hurts, and my eyes don't like the brightness, but otherwise, my brain isn't nearly as cloudy as before.

After the car accident, I passed out. I came to when I was in the back of an ambulance. I don't remember much about it, but I remember being angry that I wasn't allowed to go home.

"My mother," I say to the nurse as she stands beside my bed.

"She's here. She was admitted a few hours ago."

"Admitted?"

She nods. "She's up on the second floor."

"Is she okay?"

"I don't know. I can call up there and speak with the nurse for you."

She pulls the curtain closed, and I hear doctors and nurses tending to other patients. One man, sounding like he's right next to me, loudly moans and groans. I look in his direction but can't see anything through the curtains. Further off, I hear two muffled voices, male and female. I can't make out what they're saying.

After several minutes, my nurse returns with a man following her. He steps around her and shines a light in my eyes.

"You're looking a lot better," he says.

"What's going on with my mother?"

He turns out his light and straightens. "She's not doing well."

"How bad?"

"You'll have to ask her doctor, but it doesn't sound good."

"Is it Dr. Woodbury?"

He looks over at the nurse and she nods.

"Can I see her?"

He nods and motions to the nurse. She leaves and comes back with a wheelchair.

"I don't need that."

"If you want to go see your mother, you do," the doctor says, motioning for me to give him my hand. He helps me to my feet, then into the wheelchair. The nurse wheels me through the emergency portion of the hospital, and I see the moaner. His hand is wrapped in a large bandage, and he's holding it to his chest.

We reach the elevators, and she hits the button for the second floor. She wheels me down the hall, past several rooms, then stops and whispers to the nurse sitting at the station. "This is her daughter. Okay to go in?"

The nurse nods, and my nurse opens the door, then pushes me inside.

My mother is lying in bed, her eyes closed. She's wearing a hospital gown, and she has an IV in her arm. The TV is on, but the sound is muted. My nurse wheels me up beside the bed.

"I'm going to go see if I can get more information for you. I'll be back."

I thank her, and she leaves the room, shutting the door behind her. I lean forward and rub my mother's hand. It's enough to wake her, and her eyes flutter open. She peers at me for several seconds before recognition dawns.

"Sherry," she whispers.

"Hi, Mom."

She motions to her head, then points at me.

"It's okay. The doctor says I have a concussion, but I'm doing much better now."

She gives me a weak thumbs-up.

"Does it hurt to talk?"

She pantomimes taking a breath, and I notice the oxygen tube running to her nose.

There's a soft knock at the door, and a woman enters. She's in her mid-fifties with straight blond hair. She's quite thin. "Hi, Sherry," she says.

"Hi, Dr. Woodbury."

"How are you feeling?" she asks as she approaches and looks me over. "I understand you've had quite a day."

"Yeah. I'm feeling okay. My head hurts a little, but otherwise, pretty good."

"I heard you hit that other car pretty hard. Slippery roads out there."

I nod, and she looks at Mom. "How are you doing, Beverly? Can you breathe okay?"

Mom gives her a thumbs-up and winks at me.

Dr. Woodbury examines Mom's IV bag, then tells her she's going to talk to me for a few minutes. She then wheels me out of the room and down the hall. We enter a small room with two chairs and a table. Dr. Woodbury closes the door and turns on the lights, but I ask if she wouldn't mind keeping them off. She agrees and sits down in the chair near me.

"How is she?" I ask.

Her look is somber. "Not good. I'm afraid there's nothing else we can do for her other than keep her comfortable."

Tears spring to my eyes, and I look down. She hands me a tissue, then rubs my hand. After several seconds, I look back up. "How long?"

"Hours. Maybe a day or two at the most."

We sit in silence for several seconds.

"Do you have any questions?" Dr. Woodbury asks.

I shake my head and rub my eyes and nose with the tissue. I've known this was coming. How does a woman who has never smoked a cigarette have lung cancer?

"We're going to manage her pain. It might get a little rough. We'll do our best to keep her comfortable."

"Thank you," I whisper.

She stands and rubs my shoulder. "Do you want to go back?"

I look at my watch. Nicole is going to be out of school soon. "Do you know what happened to my car?"

She shakes her head. "I don't. But you can't drive now."

"My daughter's going to be done with school in a few minutes."

"Is there someone else who can get her?"

I pull my phone from my pocket and see that I have several missed calls. One is from the school, but they didn't leave a message. "I've got a friend I can call."

I search through my phone and find Nancy's contact. I call, and thankfully she answers. After telling her about my accident and Mom being hospitalized, I ask if she can pick up Nicole.

"Oh, hun, of course I can. When is she out?"

"In about twenty minutes."

"I'll go right now."

"Thank you."

"Do you want me to bring her there?"

"Please."

We hang up, and Dr. Woodbury wheels me back to Mom and leaves, closing the door. The TV is still on but muted. Mom was watching it when we came in but now looks at me.

"Nancy is picking up Nicole. She's bringing her here."

Mom raises her thumb.

Tears spring to my eyes, and I brush at them with my tissue. When I've got myself under control, I look back up at her.

Mom holds up a finger and takes several deep breaths. "Before she gets here, I've got something I need to say," Mom says between shallow breaths.

"Okay."

"Sherry, Nicole saw something."

I frown at her. "Saw something?"

She nods. "Play," she gasps.

"She told you that?"

She shakes her head. She holds her hand over her heart. "I know," she whispers.

We stare at each other, neither speaking.

Finally, she says, "Ron."

I frown. What does my husband have to do with this? "What about him?" I ask.

"Connected."

I shake my head. "Mom, what are you talking about? Ron died six months ago."

She stares at me. "Connected. Ron and Roy."

I stare at her, not comprehending. Ron died at our house in an accident last spring. Roy died a few days ago on a stage at the high school. How could they be connected?

I feel a buzzing in my pocket and look down and remove my phone. Nancy is calling.

"Hello? Nancy?"

"Sherry." A pause on the other end. "Look, are you sure Nicole came to school today? Did she stay home?"

I feel a jolt and grip the phone. "Yes, of course. I took her myself."

Nancy is quiet on the other end. "Sherry, nobody here has seen her today. The office says she was marked absent."

"That's impossible."

She's quiet on the other end. "You hit your head hard. You have a concussion. Maybe you're confused."

I stand up from my chair and feel a little shaky. "Nancy, I took her to school. That was before I got in my accident."

"Could she have gone back home?"

I think about our conversation in the car on the way to school. Maybe she was worried about her grandma. Maybe she left school and went back home.

"Nancy, can you go check? Can you find her?"

Chapter 22
Hank

"You know, I was thinking," Joyce says from the passenger seat of the Charger.

"You?" I say with mock surprise.

She grins. "I think I've been taking it too easy on you."

I turn the wheel and hit traffic on the corner of Holmes Avenue and First Street. There's been an accident, and an ambulance pulls up.

"Oh? Taking it easy on me, huh? How do you figure?"

She points at the dashboard. "We've been partners now for, what, a year or so?"

"A little over."

"Right. And all that time, we've been listening to the same radio station."

"That's not my fault. You won't let me change it."

She smiles. "That might have been true for the first year. But lately, you've liked it. Don't think I've missed your toe tapping or your drumming on the steering wheel."

I shrug. "Maybe, but what's your point?"

"My point is, radio stations play the same music repeatedly. They know what songs keep their listeners engaged, and they arrange their playlists to emphasize those songs."

"So?"

"So that's why I've been buying Cokes recently." She holds up her phone. "What if we changed the playlist?"

I watch her curiously as she starts playing with the settings on the radio and connects her phone to Bluetooth. A song begins to play, and she grins at me.

I chuckle. "You've got Spotify?"

"What? I can't listen to Spotify?"

I grin. "This started with you playing Elvis for Shawn, didn't it?"

"Maybe. What does that matter?"

I hold up my hands. "It doesn't. I'm just asking."

She winks. "It's even the premium subscription."

I put my hand over my chest and pretend to have a hard time breathing.

"Shut up," she says, smacking my arm. "Name the band and song."

The ambulance pulls away from the accident, and traffic begins to move. I let the car creep forward as I listen to the song.

Hey, baby, oh, baby, pretty baby
Darling, can't you do me now?
Hey, baby, oh, baby, pretty baby
Move me while you do me now
Didn't take too long 'fore I found out
What people mean by down and out

I know exactly who the band is, but not surprisingly, she's picked a song that doesn't have the title in the lyrics.

"Led Zeppelin," I say.

She nods. "Impressive, Detective. But that's only half of it."

I pull into the Albertsons parking lot and listen to the rest of the song. When it ends, she pauses the music and looks at me. "Time's up."

"It's either 'Immigrant Song' or 'Black Dog.'"

The shock on her face is priceless. She stares at me open-mouthed. Finally, she says, "You have to choose."

I trace my lips with my finger. "'Black Dog.'"

She turns away from me and gets out of the car. I shut off the engine and hustle to catch up as she walks to the entrance. She looks up at me as I grin at her.

"I'm right, aren't I?"

She shakes her head and enters the store through the automated doors. When we're beside the shopping carts, she stomps her foot and looks around. I chuckle, then laugh when she peers up at me with a disgusted expression.

Joyce growls and looks around the store, getting her bearings. I join her and see he's standing near one of the checkout counters. He's impossible to miss with those broad shoulders and stooped back. He's at least a foot taller than the woman he's talking to. She holds what looks like a receipt, pointing to something on it. We walk to them, and the conversation ends as we draw near. Our movement catches his eye, and he looks over, recognizing us.

"Hello, Detectives."

"Hello, Mr. Luelan," I say.

"You can call me Rich."

"Okay, Rich," I say, holding out my hand.

He takes it, then shakes hands with Joyce.

"You have news for me?" he asks.

I shake my head. "But, we'd like a few minutes of your time, if possible?"

He nods and tells the checkout clerk he's going to be in the office. She looks at us curiously, then we follow him to a room behind the customer service counter. He shuts the door and sits behind the desk as we sit in the chairs along the wall. It's a small office, and my shoulder leans against the door as I sit beside Joyce.

"So, what's up?"

"How are you holding up?" Joyce asks.

He shrugs. "You mean considering I have the whole town thinking I've raised a murderer? Pretty good." He chuckles sarcastically.

"Can I ask you something?" Joyce says.

He nods.

"Why haven't you posted bail to get him out?"

He laughs. "Do you know how much that judge set the bail for?"

We shake our heads.

"A million dollars. Can you believe that? A million?" He sighs. "I don't have anywhere close to that. I'm an assistant manager at a grocery store. I make sixty grand a year." He places his palm flat on the desk and looks at it. "There's nothing I can do to get him out until the trial." He looks up. "I'm glad you came by. I've been meaning to thank you for bringing him those Elvis CDs and the posters. It's really made a difference. He's much happier. Before that, I didn't think he'd make it. I still don't."

"You're welcome," Joyce says. "We're still working the case. If we can find whoever is responsible, we can get Shawn out."

Rich nods.

"Speaking of, I have a couple questions."

"Shoot."

"Do you know a man named Ed Warner?"

He frowns and pinches his lips. "Ed Warner." He shakes his head. "Doesn't ring a bell."

"You never heard Shawn talk about Ed? Maybe about a man who built the sets they used in the play?"

Rich shakes his head. "Why, is he the guy who did this?"

"We're not sure yet. We just know he provided the swords. We were hoping Shawn knew something about him."

Rich frowns. "Sorry, I can't help you there."

Joyce nods. "Do you know a girl in the class named Nicole?"

"Nicole Morgan?"

"Yes."

"Sure." Rich smiles. "Shawn calls her his girlfriend."

Roy's mom said the same thing.

"Did Shawn ever mention a secret Nicole was keeping?"

Rich starts to shake his head, then stops. "You know, I think he did. But I didn't think much of it. He was always saying things like that, and it never meant anything."

"Did he ever mention what the secret was?"

Rich shakes his head.

"Do you think Shawn knows what it is?"

There's a knock on the door, and the door presses against my arm as someone tries to push their way in. I squeeze my arms together and lean toward Joyce. A woman pokes her head in, then sees us and startles.

"Sorry, Rich. There's a problem in produce."

He looks at her warily. "It's not..."

She frowns and shakes her head. "Oh, no, nothing like that."

He nods. "Good. Thanks, Cheryl. I'm almost done here. I'll be right out."

She closes the door, and Rich stands from the desk.

"I really don't know if he knew the secret, but I can ask him later today. I'm going straight there after my shift."

He comes around the desk and opens the door.

"Did something happen in produce?" Joyce asks.

He sighs. "Remember what I said about the whole town thinking I raised a murderer?"

We both nod.

"Someone came to the store the other day and wanted to see me. When I came out he threw tomatoes at me. He told me to leave town."

"I'm sorry," I say.

He shrugs, then looks me in the eye. "Clear my boy. Let me bring him home."

"We'll do our best."

He extends his hand, and we both shake it, then walk out of the store. When we're back in the car, Joyce looks at me.

"How did you do it?"

It takes me a second to realize what she's talking about. Then I grin at her. "Do what?"

"You know what."

"Lucky guess," I say and shrug.

She doesn't need to know that when she set up her Spotify playlist, she made it public. I saw it when we were in Shawn's jail cell. I've memorized every song on that list.

Chapter 23

Sherry

"Nancy, what do you mean nobody has seen her today? I dropped her off at school. I watched her walk into the building."

Nancy is back at the high school, standing in the head office. She went to my house and couldn't find Nicole. I told her to return and call me when she arrived.

"Sherry, I'm standing here in the office with the principal. Nicole wasn't in class today."

"Let me talk to him."

I stand out of the wheelchair and walk to the window in my mother's hospital room. I look out as Principal Skinner comes on the line.

"Sherry, nobody has seen her today. We assumed you left her home again."

"What do you mean, 'left her home?'"

"The other day in the office, you said you didn't want her coming back until she was safe."

"Yes, and then I brought her back. She was in class yesterday."

"Sherry, I'm going to put you on speaker. Georgette just came in."

There's a shuffle noise, then I hear a door shut.

"Sherry?" It's the voice of Nicole's teacher, Georgette Thomas.

"Yes, I'm here. Where's Nicole, Georgette?"

"She wasn't in class?"

"That's impossible," I shout. The dam of emotions breaks, and tears pour down my face. "She was there." I sob. "I dropped her off. I watched her walk into the building."

"Sherry, we're going to check the security camera footage and make an announcement. We'll get everyone looking for her. We've already called the police," Principal Skinner says.

I turn away from the window and look at my dying mother. She has hours to live, and I've got a dilemma.

"Nancy?" I say.

"I'm here, Sherry."

"Can you come get me from the hospital? I'm at Eastern Idaho Medical Center."

"Absolutely. I'll be right there."

Chapter 24
Hank

As we pull into the station parking lot, several marked cars exit from behind the gate and turn on their sirens. We watch them go, looking at each other, then park and exit the car. We enter the building and find Officer Levy waiting for us just inside the front doors. She's reading something on her phone and looks up when she sees us.

"Hi, detectives."

"Hello, Carol," Joyce says, motioning behind her with her thumb. "Where are they going?"

She holds up her phone. "Just got a call from the high school. I guess there's a missing student."

Joyce looks at me, then back at Levy. "At Skyline?"

She nods and looks past us. We turn and see Captain Rigby striding down the hallway. He points at us, then beckons us to follow. I raise my eyebrows at Levy, then fall in line behind Joyce as she walks to the captain's office. When we reach it, he's already seated behind his desk.

"Sit down," he says, pointing to the chairs.

We take our usual spots.

"I hear you two have been spending a lot of time at the high school."

Neither of us speaks.

"Do you have anything new?"

I shake my head while Joyce sits with her arms crossed.

"I got a call from the principal a few minutes ago. He asked that you not come back. He says you've been scaring some of the kids. I guess one of the kids you've been talking to didn't show up today and is lost. I just sent officers to help them find her."

"One we've been talking to?" Joyce asks.

"Yes, in the special class."

"Which kid?" I ask.

"A girl. I guess her mother has been threatening to sue the school over the murder. She was onstage when it happened."

"Nicole Morgan?" I say.

He nods, and Joyce and I sit forward in our chairs.

"What do you mean, 'lost'?" Joyce says.

Captain Rigby frowns, noticing our reaction. "I don't know all the details. Some of our officers are investigating. Sounds like she went to school but disappeared sometime during the day. The principal thinks she ran off because of you."

We're a long way from the front doors of the building, but even from here we can hear shouting. All of us stand and walk into the hall. Officer Levy is trying to calm someone who has just come through the doors. She's screaming, and although she's far away, I can tell who it is. She's joined by another woman who seems uncertain about what to do.

"Ma'am, you need to calm down," Officer Levy says as we grow closer.

When we're twenty feet away, with Joyce in front, Sherry Morgan turns and sees us.

"It's your fault," she screams, pointing at Joyce and rushing toward her.

I step in front of her and catch her hands. She's fighting me off, tears streaming down her face. "Nicole's gone because of you. They killed her, just like Roy." She stops fighting me and sinks to her knees on the floor. "They have my baby."

Chapter 25

Sherry

I can't stop shaking, and with every minute, the tremor becomes more pronounced. After screaming at Detective Powers, Detective Gardner picked me up and put me into this room. He told me to "cool down," then locked the door. Nancy came with me, and now she's sitting at my side, rubbing my shoulder and telling me it's going to be okay. The tears have stopped, and all I feel now is a numbing frost emanating from my extremities.

"Is it cold in here?" I ask through chattering teeth.

She's been looking at me the same way since she picked me up at the hospital—that same vertical line running down the middle of her forehead.

"Do you want a blanket?"

I nod, and she goes to the door and knocks. After several seconds, the female cop who tried to hold me back at the building entrance opens the door.

"Can we get a blanket?" Nancy asks.

Her eyes flash to me. "Sure. Just a minute."

She closes the door, and I hear it lock.

Nancy looks up at the ceiling, then after a few seconds, down at her shoes.

After a minute, the door opens, bumping into her. Detectives Powers and Gardner enter the room. Detective Powers holds a blanket and offers it to Nancy. Nancy thanks her and comes around the table and wraps it over my shoulders, then sits back down. The detectives watch me, then sit at the opposite side of the table. I find their stares unnerving.

"Mrs. Morgan," Detective Gardner says. "We're doing everything we can to find your daughter. We're hopeful she'll be returned to you safe and sound. For that to happen, we need some help from you. We have some questions."

I've been focusing on Detective Powers but look away from her to him, then back.

"You knew," I say with a nod. My words are as cold as I feel. I point a finger at her. "You knew you were putting her in danger by visiting our house, yet you did it anyway."

Detective Powers says nothing.

Detective Gardner clears his throat. "Mrs. Morgan, our intention was never to put your daughter in danger. Our job was to investigate a murder. That's what we did. That's what we're still doing."

I shake my head. "No," I exclaim and slap the table. "Don't give me that BS. She knew what she was doing. She made a choice to endanger my daughter, and because of that, Nicole is missing or..." A sob escapes my lips before I can finish. I grab a tissue and fight to control my emotions. I wipe my nose and eyes, and see she's still just watching me. Her hands are on the table, and she's lightly drumming her fingernails.

"Sherry," Detective Gardner says. "Believe me when I tell you, you want Detective Powers on this case. If anyone can bring Nicole home, it's her."

Detective Powers remains silent, her eyes boring into me.

Feeling as if I have no other choice, I wave a hand and tell him to ask his questions.

He opens the file he's been holding and uncaps a pen. "Let's start with some basic information. Nicole's date of birth?"

"July 11, 2007."

"Full name?"

"Nicole Morgan."

"No middle name?"

I shake my head.

"Height."

"I don't know. You saw her. Short. Barely over four feet."

"Weight?"

"Just over a hundred pounds."

"Tell us about today. What happened?"

I tell him about being late for school. About dropping Nicole off and allowing her to enter the school herself because of my mother's health. I talk about my rush to get back to my mother and then the car accident.

"You're sure you saw her enter the school?" he asks.

"Yes, positive."

"Was anyone else there? Did you see anyone?"

I shake my head. "Nobody. It was deserted. School already started."

Detective Powers holds up a hand, and everyone looks at her. "Did you ask her?"

I stare at her, not sure what she's referring to. "Ask her what?"

"Did she have a secret?"

I shake my head in frustration. "No, I was planning to after school."

Detective Powers frowns and looks back at Detective Gardner.

"But she asked me about secrets," I say.

Both detectives focus back on me.

"What did she say?" Detective Gardner asks.

"She asked if secrets were bad."

"That's how she said it?" Detective Powers asks. "Are secrets bad?"

I nod.

"What did you say?" she asks.

"I said they can be, but sometimes we keep secrets to not hurt others." I brush my nose with the tissue. "I thought she might have been talking about me. I never told her how sick her grandmother was. I don't know why, but I got the feeling she was talking about that. That I was keeping a secret from her."

"And you still have no idea if she was holding a secret?" Detective Gardner asks.

I shake my head.

"We're going to issue a purple alert for her," Detective Gardner says.

"What's that?" Nancy asks.

I look over at her, surprised she spoke.

Detective Gardner glances at her. "It's like an Amber Alert, but for those who are adults and may not be able to care for themselves. Typically, those with cognitive disabilities." He looks back at me. "It will help get the word out. The good and bad of it is that it's going to alert the media. Don't be surprised if you see news crews in your neighborhood."

The detectives stand, and Detective Gardner opens the door.

"Where are you going?" I ask.

"To the school," Detective Gardner says.

"What about us? Where should we go?"

Detective Powers answers. "Go back to the hospital, and be with your mom. We'll call you if anything comes up."

Chapter 26
Hank

I park the car, and we get out, walking toward the front doors of the high school. Although it's barely five p.m., the sun has almost set over the mountains to the west, and the temperature has dropped. Several police cars are parked in front, and Officer Levy exits the high school and cuts us off before entering the building.

"What's up, Carol?" Joyce asks as we approach.

She motions with her head back to the school. "The principal, two teachers, and the school counselor are waiting for you inside the head office. Trevor had them pull the video surveillance from the cameras in the school. He's reviewing them now. Captain Rigby asked me to organize a neighborhood search. We've got officers in cars canvassing the area."

"Is the captain here?" Joyce asks, looking around.

She shakes her head. "He called."

Joyce grunts, and we walk past Levy, then Joyce stops and turns back.

"Hey, Carol?"

"Yes?"

"I'm surprised the purple alert hasn't been sent yet. Do you know what the holdup is?"

She looks at her watch. "It should go out any second now. I guess because they're less frequent than Amber or Silver, they had to check terms and conditions with Legal."

Joyce nods and looks around the school. "When it does, expect the public to start showing up. Better tape off the front here and post a couple officers."

Levy nods, and we walk into the building. We enter the office and find a table has been moved to the center. Principal Skinner, Georgette Thomas, Lucrezia Ferguson, and Jim Roberts sit around it. I look to the right and see Trevor, our IT analyst, sitting at the computer normally occupied by Brenda Wallace, the school office secretary. He sees us and waves. We smile a greeting and then pull up chairs at the table and sit down.

"You've got a lot going on here, Principal," Joyce says, looking at him.

It's the first time I've ever seen him without a suit coat. His blue shirt is untucked on one side, and his tie is loosened with the top button on his collar undone. Sweat stains are visible on his shirt under the arms.

He says nothing as I put a file on the table and uncap my pen.

"I don't think it needs to be said, but I'm going to say it anyway," Joyce says. "Nicole Morgan is likely in grave danger. The faster we find her, the better. Did anyone see her at the school today?"

She looks from person to person as they all shake their heads.

"From what we understand, nobody has seen her since her mother dropped her off this morning. Nicole entered," Joyce turns and points to the outside doors, "right over there. Do you know of anyone who saw her enter this morning?"

Again, they all shake their heads.

"What about Mrs. Wallace? She didn't see her?" Joyce asks.

Skinner clears his throat. "She wasn't here. She was late today. She had trouble with her car because of the snow."

Joyce and I look at each other, and I make a note.

"What time did she arrive?" Joyce asks.

Skinner shrugs. "Maybe thirty minutes after school started."

Joyce frowns. "So, who was in the office when Nicole arrived?"

"I don't think anyone," he says.

"Where were you?"

"I got a text from the janitor saying someone broke into the cafeteria and made a mess all over the floor. They wrote a message in ketchup and mustard."

Joyce frowns. "They broke into the school to leave a message? They didn't take anything or break anything?"

Skinner shakes his head.

"What did the message say?"

"Skinner sucks."

Lucrezia Ferguson stifles a laugh and looks up at the ceiling. Skinner shoots her a withering glance.

"That's nothing new. The joy of being a high school principal, I guess."

"There have been other 'Skinner sucks' messages?" Joyce asks, putting a hand over her mouth to hide her smile.

He nods.

Joyce drops her hand. "Okay, so you went down to the cafeteria to read your love note and left the office open and empty?"

Everyone but Skinner is smiling now. Even Georgette Thomas.

Skinner looks around the table. "I'm glad you all think it's funny." He leans forward and drops his head. "No."

"No, what?" Joyce asks.

"It wasn't empty."

"Who was here?"

"Penny."

"Who's Penny?"

"She's a high school girl who helps out during first period."

I make a note.

"So, Penny was in the office?"

"Yes."

"Where is Penny now?" Joyce asks.

"Home."

"How do you know she didn't see Nicole?"

"Because she said so. At lunch, Georgette, I mean Ms. Thomas, told me Nicole wasn't in school. I called her home, I mean her mom, to check on her, but she never answered. I asked Penny if she saw her, and she said no."

"Is that normal?" Joyce asks.

"What?"

Joyce chews on her lip. "Why would you ask a student if they had seen a girl who was marked absent for the day?"

"What do you mean?"

Joyce leans back in her chair. "That doesn't make sense to me. You already knew she wasn't in school. What would make you think Penny saw her?"

Skinner sits back in his chair and swallows. "Because her mom was threatening to sue the school after what happened at the play. I've been keeping a close eye on her. Her mom wasn't going to let her come back to school, then she did, and I got worried when she wasn't here again."

"Hmm," Joyce says and crosses her arms.

"Where's Mrs. Wallace?" I ask. "Why isn't she here?"

"She had a piano recital for one of her daughters. She left a few minutes ago."

I make a note. "Do you know anyone who would want to hurt Nicole?"

They all shake their heads.

"So, the last time you saw her was yesterday?"

They all nod.

Joyce drums her fingernails on the table. "All right, if you were forced to guess where Nicole is, what would you say?" She points to Ms. Thomas. "Let's start with you."

Georgette Thomas shakes her head. "I don't know."

"That's not an option," Joyce says. "Give me your best guess."

Ms. Thomas looks at Skinner, then back at Joyce. "If I had to guess, I'd say she either ran away or went back home or went to a neighbor's house. Hasn't her mother been in the hospital today?"

Joyce nods.

"Maybe that's it. She's lost."

Joyce watches her for several seconds, then turns to Lucrezia Ferguson.

"Same," she says.

Joyce turns to the school counselor, Mr. Roberts.

He shrugs. "I don't know."

"Not an option," Joyce says.

He takes a deep breath. "Maybe someone took her," he says and shrugs.

Joyce looks at Skinner. "What about you, Principal?"

Skinner rubs his forehead. "She's been through a lot lately with her dad dying and now Roy. Maybe something spooked her and she ran away."

"Ran away to where?" Joyce asks.

He shakes his head.

Both Joyce and I stare at him, forcing him to answer.

"Maybe she's hiding back home." He motions to Ms. Thomas. "Or maybe she's with a friend or neighbor, like Georgette said."

Out of the corner of my eye, I see that Trevor is standing beside the table. Joyce and I look up at him.

"Detectives." He motions with his head. "Can I see you for a minute?"

We stand and follow him out into the school lobby. The lobby is empty, but he still motions us away from the office. He's a young kid, barely out of college.

"There's something wrong with the video footage," he says in a hushed voice.

"What do you mean?" Joyce says. "Did you see something?"

He shakes his head. "It's what I didn't see."

"What do you mean?" I ask.

"Someone disconnected the camera here at the front of the school. At the entrance."

Chapter 27
Sherry

I sit in the faux-leather chair beside the window in my mother's hospital room and scroll through my phone, searching for anybody who might have seen my daughter. After leaving the police headquarters, Nancy dropped me off here and went to my house. She promised to stay there, waiting in case Nicole came home.

I stop at the first name in my directory and type a generic message, then copy and paste it into text message threads over and over.

Hello, this is Sherry Morgan. I don't know if you've heard, but my daughter, Nicole Morgan, is missing. She was last seen at Skyline High School this morning. If you've seen her or have any information about her disappearance, please contact me. I'm desperate to find her.

With each text, I include the most recent picture I have of her. She's wearing her Christine outfit right before her performance in *The Phantom of the Opera*. When I reach the end of my list, I flip to social media and post the same message along with the same picture of her. Almost immediately, messages flood my phone. People want to know what happened and how they can help. So many messages come in, I can't respond to all of them.

There's a knock at the door, and my mother stirs. I go to the door and open it. My neighbor from across the street, Lisa Young, stands at the door with a balloon and flowers.

"Lisa, hi."

"Hi, Sherry. Sorry to intrude. I just wanted to come by and check on you guys. How's she doing?"

"Not good."

She nods. "I saw the ambulance. I hope you don't mind that I came by."

"Please," I say, opening the door wider and motioning to her. "Come in. She's sleeping."

Lisa enters and approaches the bed. She looks down at Mom. Mom's eyes open, and I see she recognizes her. Mom reaches out, and Lisa takes her hand. In her other hand, she still holds the flowers and balloon. Seeing she's trying to find somewhere for them, I take them from her and put them on the table beside the window. Lisa stands over the bed, leaning against the rail.

"How are you doing, Beverly?"

Mom flashes her eyes at me.

"It's hard for her to talk," I say. "She's in pain, and her breathing is getting more difficult."

Lisa looks grave, then turns back to Mom. "Oh, Beverly, I'm so sorry."

Mom shrugs. "Thank you," she whispers.

There's an awkward pause, and I ask Lisa if she'd like to sit. I take my place back against the window, and Lisa sits in one of the plastic chairs along the bathroom wall.

"I appreciate you coming," I say and look at Mom. "She does too. Thank you."

"Of course. Do you need anything?" She looks around the room. "Where's Nicole?"

I watch her eyes come back to me. The question is innocent. She doesn't know.

"Didn't you get my text?"

She shakes her head and looks down, searching for her purse as I look at my phone. Notifications cover the locked screen. I have scores of unread messages. Momentarily, I worried the messages hadn't gone through, but that can't be. Lisa opens her purse, finds her phone, and reads my message. Her head whips up, and her eyes register shock. She fumbles over her words, trying to find something to say.

"Sherry, I... Oh, I...I'm so sorry. You must have texted while I was in the car."

I shake my head and extend my trembling hand to her. "It's okay. I'm relieved to see you got the message. When I opened the door, I wasn't sure if that was why you came."

"It wasn't. I mean...obviously. How? I mean, what happened?"

I shake my head, tears edging my eyelids. "I dropped her off at school this morning. I saw her walk in, but nobody has seen her since." I look over at Mom and see she's back asleep.

"What can I do?" Lisa asks.

I shake my head. "I don't know. Do you have any ideas?"

She's an older woman in her early sixties. She raised three kids who are all out of the house and raising families of their own. Her husband works as an accountant at a local firm. She teaches music at the elementary school across town.

"Did they catch anything on camera?" she asks.

"Camera?"

She nods. "Most schools have security cameras in high-traffic areas, like near the outside doors or common areas. Did they check those?"

I shake my head. "I don't know. I haven't heard. I talked to the police, then came here." I look back at Mom.

"Of course." She stands and picks up her purse. "Let me go by the school. Maybe I can get more information for you. I'll see what I can find out. Maybe I can organize a neighborhood search party. Has anyone done that yet?"

I stand and walk with her. "I don't know. I've been here."

She nods and stops walking, hugging me, then pulls back and holds my hand. She looks into my eyes. "Sherry, we're going to find her. Everything is going to be okay."

Her reassurance does something to me. As I look into her eyes, for the first time since I received the news, I have hope.

Lisa turns away and heads for the door. Before she reaches it, she turns back. "Did you check with Ed? Has he seen her?"

I frown. "Who?"

"Ed Warner. He lives behind you. I've seen Nicole outside talking to him several times. She's always showing him her music. When he first moved in, I saw her bike at his house."

I take a step toward her. "What?"

She frowns. "You didn't know? I just assumed... Oh, I'm sorry, Sherry. I thought you knew." She shakes her head and puts her hand on my shoulder. "Don't worry. He seems very nice. I'm not sure that I have his number, but I'll stop by his house on the way to the school. I'll ask him if he's seen her."

I nod, my mind racing. "Thank you."

She closes the door, and I look at my mother. When would Nicole have talked to Ed? When did she see him? Her bike was at his house? When? Why?

I rush back to my phone and grab the card on the seat beside the window. I punch in the numbers and hear ringing on the other end.

Chapter 28

Hank

Trevor walks back into the head office, and Joyce and I remain in the lobby. Simultaneously, our phones ping, and we pull them out and check them.

"There's the purple alert," I say.

She nods and scrolls through notifications, then puts her phone away and looks up at me. "It's going to get crazy now."

"Hopefully, someone will have seen her."

"I hope so," she says, putting her hands on her hips and looking at the front doors.

Both of our eyes move up to the camera in the corner, just to the side of the entrance. I know she's thinking the same thing I am. Someone was planning this. Which means we were right about Shawn. Someone planted that sword. They wanted Roy dead, and now they have Nicole. She's in real danger, which means she did have a secret.

My phone buzzes, and I look at the caller ID. It's Sherry Morgan. I show it to Joyce, then answer.

"Hi, Sherry. How's your mom?"

She sounds frantic. "Detective Gardner?"

"Yes."

"My neighbor Lisa Young just came to the hospital. She told me she saw Nicole with Ed Warner, another neighbor, multiple times. Her bike was at his house."

"When was her bike at his house? Today?"

"No. Other times. I didn't know about it. She must have gone when I was away. Has Lisa come by the school yet?"

"No."

"She just left here. Maybe she went to Ed's house first. She was going to go talk to him and see if he had seen Nicole."

"By herself?"

"I think so. Why?"

"I don't think it's good for anyone to be alone right now. Okay. This is good information. We'll go and talk to him with her."

Joyce looks at me, frowning, and I hold up a finger.

"Okay, good. Lisa mentioned something while she was here. She works in the elementary school and asked if you've checked the surveillance cameras yet."

"Yes, we have."

"Did you find anything?"

I consider how to answer this. "No. The cameras didn't pick up anything."

"Nothing?" she asks desperately.

"No, I'm sorry. I'll let you know how things go with Ed Warner. Get back to your mom. We'll keep you informed."

I end the call and look at Joyce. "A neighbor came by the hospital and told her she saw Nicole talking to Ed Warner multiple times. She saw her bike parked there in the past. The neighbor, Lisa, is going over to check if Ed has seen Nicole."

"Let's go," Joyce says and strides for the doors, then stops. She holds up a finger. "Not just yet. I've got to ask Skinner one more thing."

I follow back into the office. The three school employees sit around the desk, whispering when we walk in. Joyce heads straight to Skinner. "Who set up your security cameras?"

Skinner looks bewildered and leans back. "I don't know. Someone from the district."

"Who checked the cameras? Who made sure they were working?"

"Me or sometimes Brenda."

Joyce turns and points behind her but keeps her eyes on him. "Did you know this one was disconnected?"

He swallows and shakes his head.

She glares at him in disgust. "You had someone break in. Just yesterday? How did you not check the cameras?"

He raises his hands, palms up. "There's no camera back by the cafeteria where they broke in. There wasn't any point."

Her voice rises, and she shouts, "How about now? Is there a point now?"

I reach for her arm and pull her with me toward the door. "Come on, Joyce."

She retreats, walking backward, keeping her eyes on him until we reach the door. I wave goodbye to Trevor. He's back working on the computer. I open the door and guide Joyce out.

When we're outside, we pass two uniformed officers. Caution tape surrounds the front of the building, and we duck under it. I'm surprised to see no one from the community has come to the school. Maybe it's the bitter cold, especially with the sun now down.

After we get in the car, Joyce says, "Bart Simpson was right."

"Huh?" I say, turning the wheel and pulling out onto the street. I glance over at her.

"Skinner does suck."

We smile at each other.

"What are the chances?" I say.

"What? That your name is Seymour Skinner and you become a principal?"

I laugh. "Yeah. I mean, I think I would have picked a different profession."

She tilts her head and looks out the window. "Maybe that's why he became a principal. It might tell us something about his personality."

I rub my chin with my left hand while keeping my right on the steering wheel. Snow is beginning to fall, and I worry about the Charger slipping. We get to the neighborhood, and I see a red Honda CR-V pull into the driveway behind the brown Silverado. Lisa, the neighbor, gets out of the car, and I pull up behind her while Joyce rolls down her window.

"Mrs. Young," Joyce calls out as Lisa steps from her vehicle. She looks at us curiously. Joyce waves her over, but she doesn't come and instead looks at the house. "Lisa," Joyce calls, holding up her badge. Lisa squints to see it in the dark, then comes forward.

"Sherry called us," Joyce says. "We appreciate your information, but why don't you let us take it from here?"

"Oh...okay. Do you want me to go?" she asks, pointing to her car.

"That would probably be best."

She nods and gets back in her car while I park beside the curb and we get out. She pulls out of the driveway as we walk up, past the Silverado. We take a moment to shine our lights into the back and inside the cab. The back is full of construction material. The cab is covered with dog hair and trash.

We reach the front door, and I knock loudly. A small dog barks from behind the door. After several seconds, the door opens, and Ed Warner stands holding his beagle in his arms. The dog howls at us and fights to get free.

"Hello, Edward," Joyce says. "Remember us?"

He looks at us warily. "Yeah."

"Do you mind if we come in?"

He takes a hand off the dog and grips the door. The dog senses an opportunity and wiggles free, landing on the wood floor. He spins around, howling.

"Domo," Ed scolds, looking down at the dog.

The dog stops spinning and continues to howl, backing up as he does it.

Ed still grips the door with his right hand. He looks back at us. "What's this about?"

"We just have a few more questions for you," Joyce says.

He looks at her, then at me, and grips the door harder. "You can ask your questions from right there."

Joyce glares at him. "You lied to us, Ed. You knew Nicole. You knew her very well. She was seen here at your house on several occasions."

"No," he says, shaking his head and swallowing.

"I'm afraid so," Joyce says. "We have witnesses who saw her here."

He shakes his head. The dog stops barking and stands watching the interchange.

"Ed, did you know Nicole is missing?"

He shakes his head.

"Have you seen her today?"

He swallows, then shakes his head again.

"We're searching all the houses in the neighborhood. As you can imagine, her mom is desperate to find her. Do you mind if we come in and search your house?"

"You got a warrant?"

"Do we need one?" Joyce asks, stepping closer to him. "Are you hiding something?"

"No. But you can't come barging into private citizens' homes, you know?"

"We're just looking for a missing girl, Edward. Do we need to start asking more questions about you? If we leave and get a warrant, we're going to turn your house and property inside out."

Ed debates this, then opens his door wider. "Fine. Go ahead and look. She's not here."

We step inside, and I notice that all the decor is Western. He has several deer and elk heads mounted on the wall. We look around the front room, open the closet door, then walk to the back of the house. The kitchen has dishes in the sink and on the counter. I'd describe the house as cluttered but not nearly as bad as I thought we might find by looking in the truck. Ed follows us, holding the dog. We walk down the hall, opening closets and entering rooms. The bathroom hasn't been cleaned in months, if not years. There's a brown ring around the toilet and the sinks. The mirror is blotched with specks of toothpaste and shaving cream.

We reach the master bedroom, and there are no sheets and several brown stains on the mattress. I look down and see that the stains aren't exclusive to the mattress. The carpet is also stained, but I know what blood looks like, even when it's dry, and this isn't it. Joyce opens the closet while I hang back, keeping my eyes on Ed. He's clearly nervous. There's something here he doesn't want us to find. She checks under the bed but sees nothing suspicious.

Outside the bedroom, there's a set of stairs leading to the basement. Joyce eyes them, then goes down first, flipping on the light. I wait for Ed to go next. I want him between us. In the basement, there's a large TV room with a leather sofa and a coffee table made from animal horns. The room isn't clean, but it's less "lived in" than the rest of the house. Above one wall, there's a picture of a golden palace somewhere in Asia. Beside the picture, on the wall, there are several hooks with nothing attached to them.

"What was hanging here?" Joyce asks.

"Nothin'," Ed says.

Joyce approaches the wall, examining it. "No. There was something here. There's a definite shadow on the wall."

She turns around and looks at him.

He shakes his head, but his eyes deceive him. He looks behind her at the closet door.

Joyce follows his eyes and steps toward it.

Instinctively, he takes several steps toward her.

"Stay right there," I command, pulling out my gun and holding it on him.

His eyes go wide, and he raises his hands, dropping the dog.

The dog approaches the door and scratches at it.

Joyce watches, then looks at Ed. His eyes are down. He won't look at her.

Joyce opens the door and shines her light within. She steps back so I can see that, once again, Ed has lied to us.

Chapter 29
Sherry

The nurse comes into the room and points to Mom. "How is she?" she whispers.

Mom hasn't been awake since Lisa first arrived. The doctor warned me she would sleep more and more, and I'm sure whatever pain medication they're giving her makes her very drowsy.

I shrug. "It's hard to tell. She seems to be doing okay."

"Good. Let me know if you need anything." She examines my eyes. "How's your head?"

I absentmindedly touch my temple. "Better. Thank you."

"Do you need anything for it?"

"Not right now. I'll let you know if I do."

She nods and closes the door, and I go back to watching the TV. The ten o'clock news is about to start, and I wonder if they'll talk about Nicole. After several commercials, the lead-in for the top stories starts, and Skyline High School is the first image on the screen. There's caution tape surrounding the front of the building and several police cars. The news anchors, a male and a female, are now on the screen. The male speaks with a somber expression. He reminds everyone of the murder on the stage earlier in the week and the possible connection to Nicole's disappearance. He says they have a reporter live at the high school, and the screen flips to a man in a blue news jacket holding a microphone standing in front of the camera. The high school is behind him and looks deserted. The reporter's name is Ethan Stone.

"Ethan," the news anchor says, "what can you tell us about Nicole Morgan's disappearance?"

Ethan nods, looking serious. "Yes, Alan. As you can see behind me, this is Skyline High School. The school where Nicole Morgan is a senior in the special education classroom." He turns to the side and points to the front doors. "This is the front of the school where, earlier this morning, after her mother dropped her off, Nicole Morgan entered and then seems to have vanished." He squares his shoulders to the camera. "Nobody at the school saw her all day. She was marked absent in her classes. And since early this morning, she's been missing. Now that the school is on winter break, and students won't be returning until next year, some are wondering if her disappearance is related."

The screen moves to a picture-in-picture with Ethan and the anchor.

"Ethan," the anchor says, "is it possible the mother is mistaken? Could Nicole never have entered?"

"Alan, at this point, police are leaving open all possibilities."

"Do the police have any leads? What efforts are being made to find Nicole?"

Ethan shakes his head. "That's the trouble. There's not much to go on, unfortunately. She seems to have disappeared. The police are conducting house-to-house searches and asking anybody who may have information about Nicole to contact them."

"Ethan, did you say Nicole has special needs?"

He nods. "That's right, Alan. She is."

"What kind of disabilities does she have? Could her disappearance be related?"

Ethan shakes his head. "I asked Captain Rigby, the police chief, about that. He said it's unlikely. Nicole has never gone missing before."

The female news anchor jumps in. "Ethan, this is Brenda. Are there concerns this might be related to the death of the boy at the play several nights ago?"

Ethan tilts his head and puts his thumb and index finger together while pointing them at the camera. "The police aren't saying that. But they also aren't ruling that out."

Back to Alan. "What about the family? Where are they in all of this?"

Ethan nods. "A few minutes ago, I spoke with a neighbor who confirmed an ambulance was at the Morgan home earlier in the day. Police won't confirm it, but I'm hearing Nicole's elderly grandmother is currently hospitalized in serious condition."

Alan's mouth opens in shock. "Could that be related?"

Ethan shakes his head. "Hard to say, but it does make you wonder."

"Hmm," Brenda says.

Alan looks at her and nods, then looks back at the camera. "Thank you, Ethan. Stay warm. Let's hope they locate Nicole soon. The community is facing a bitter holiday if she's not found."

The camera switches to a close-up of Alan, and a scrolling graphic appears below him.

"As Ethan mentioned, the police are asking for your help in locating Nicole Morgan. If you have any information, you are encouraged to call the number listed on the screen below."

The camera pans back to both anchors sitting at the desk, looking at each other.

"Let's hope she's found soon," Brenda says and Alan nods.

I glance at my mother and see that her eyes are open and she's watching TV. I hit the mute button and go to her, leaning over the rail of the bed.

"How are you doing?" I ask.

She points at the TV.

"Sorry, did it wake you?"

She moves her head from side to side.

I can see she wants to say something but is struggling. Her breathing is more labored.

"What is it, Mom?"

She tries to talk, but the sounds come out in bursts. I can't make them out.

"What?"

She shakes her head in frustration and tries to push up in bed but doesn't have the strength. She takes several quick breaths, then tries again. "Go," she says and points to the door.

"Mom, I can't go. I've got to stay here with you."

She shakes her head.

I feel like I'm in an impossible situation. "Mom, what can I do? I don't know where she is. Nobody does."

My mother takes several quick breaths, then forces out the words. "Find her."

We stare at each other for several seconds, and I can see the intensity in her eyes. Finally, I nod. I turn away when her grip on my arm pulls me back. I stare down at her.

"Sherry," she whispers, barely audible. I lean in closer and see tears in her eyes. "Tell her I loved her."

Chapter 30

Sherry

"How is she?" Nancy asks as I climb into the car.

I shake my head. "She's asleep again. Talking that much took it out of her."

Nancy reaches out and pats my hand, and we drive for several minutes in silence, lost in our thoughts.

Finally, the question that's been rolling around in my head comes out. "Where is she?" I say more to myself than to Nancy. "Why would they take her?"

Nancy looks over at me and shakes her head.

We reach my house, and Nancy pulls into the driveway and cuts the engine. She turns in her seat so she can look right at me. Her face is illuminated by the light on the car ceiling.

"Sherry?"

"Hmm?"

"Lisa Young organized a search group. They've been going house to house, asking people if they've seen Nicole. They stopped about thirty minutes ago. It's late and cold. They decided to rest and come back in the morning." She stops, and I wonder what she wants me to say. "It's time you got some rest too."

I frown and shake my head, but she reaches out and grabs my hand. "Sherry, there's nothing you can do tonight. You're running on fumes."

I want to argue with her, but her look of resolve stops me. We stare at each other for several seconds, and emotion overcomes me again. She sees it and awkwardly wraps her arms around me, reaching across the car. I release big, racking sobs as I cry into her shoulder. After several seconds, I control my emotions and wipe my eyes.

"What if she's out in the cold somewhere? What if she's lost? I've got to find her."

Nancy shakes her head. "Sherry, she's not lost. The camera was disconnected at the school. That means someone took her. And if they took her, I don't believe they intended to hurt her. They're holding her for some reason. She's okay. I just know it."

"How?"

She puts her hand over her chest. "I feel it, and so do you."

I raise my fingers to my lips as I search her eyes. I can feel them tremble, then stop. Maybe it's exhaustion. Maybe it's my body trying to convince my mind, but a feeling comes over me. It's an assurance that she's right.

She puts her hand on my shoulder. "Get some rest, and everything will be better tomorrow."

She nods, and I return the gesture.

"Do you want me to stay over tonight?"

I shake my head. "No. Go home. I'll call you if anything comes up."

I open the car door, and the wind nearly blows it shut. I climb out, careful not to slip on the ice. Someone shoveled my walk and driveway. There's no snow, but there is ice from my decision to drive over the snow earlier today.

I turn back to say goodbye before she drives away, but she's not in the car. She's walking around it toward me. She holds out the keys, and I take them from her, confused.

"You might need to leave suddenly. I'd feel more comfortable if my car were here tonight. But promise me you'll only use it in an emergency."

"I promise."

She nods. "Get some rest, okay?"

I agree and we embrace.

Nancy walks down the driveway and turns toward her house as I climb my front steps and enter the house through the front door. Silence greets me, and I turn on the light and go upstairs. I look at the kitchen and wonder when I last ate. Yesterday, maybe? I consider going to the fridge and looking for something but decide against it. I don't have any appetite.

I walk down the hall and stop at Nicole's room before I can reach my own. I turn on the light and see her empty bed, and the image breaks my heart. I turn away and go to my room, strip off my clothes, and enter the bathroom. I plug in my phone, turn on the shower, and let the warm water cover my body.

After fifteen minutes, I turn off the water and dress. I brush my teeth and stare into the mirror when a thought pops into my head. The detectives said Nicole had a secret. If that was true, that had to be the reason she was taken. If I can learn the secret, I might learn who took her.

I exit the bathroom and reenter Nicole's bedroom. I open each of her drawers, pulling out her clothes and going through the pockets. I search the closet and under her bed. I find a stack of pictures she's drawn, but none of them make sense. They're of stick figures in front of a house and at a school. With each passing minute, my hope fades. There's nothing. No clues. Nothing that could be a secret.

I sit on her bed and look around. I pick her pillow off the mattress and run my hands along the sheet. I hold the pillow to my nose, smelling her scent, and curl up on the bed. Within seconds, I fade to sleep.

Chapter 31

Hank

"You ready?" Joyce asks me with her fingers on the handle of the interview-room door. I finish reading the sheet of information in the file folder and nod. She opens the door, and Ed Warner sits at the table with his arms behind his back. Joyce takes a chair opposite him, while I walk over and release the handcuffs from his wrists.

"You got no right. You know?" Ed says when his arms are free.

I sit down beside Joyce on the other side of the table. I open the file and look it over, then gaze at him. "We do have a right, actually. A sword, identical to the one used to kill Roy Edwards, was found in your house. That means you're the one who gave Shawn the sword that killed Roy. You were behind it."

Ed's face turns red. "Uh, no. Someone stole it from my house, and stuff and whatever."

"Someone stole it?"

He nods. "Damn right."

"When?"

He raises his hands. "Not sure."

"When did you notice it missing?" I ask.

He looks at me, then at Joyce, and shrugs.

I look at Joyce and chuckle. "Oh, Ed. You aren't helping your case, buddy."

"It wasn't me," he says, leaning forward. "Someone stole it from my house."

I give him a doubtful expression. "They stole it from your house? Who? When? Ed, you can't even tell me when you found it was missing."

"The other day."

"What other day?"

Ed shrugs. "The day the kid got killed. Saw it on TV."

"You saw it, then what?"

"Went downstairs and seen it was missing."

"Is that why you took the other one off the wall and put it into your storage closet?"

He nods.

I turn and look at Joyce as if Ed isn't even in the room. "Here's my problem. Ed has a real problem with telling the truth. Have you noticed that?"

Joyce nods.

"When we talked to him the other day in the house he was working in, he told us he didn't know about Roy being killed. Do you remember that?"

She nods, then looks at him. I follow her gaze back to Ed.

"What else are you lying about, Ed?" I ask in a hard tone.

He swallows and sits back in his chair, crossing his arms.

"Why didn't you go to the performance that night? Did you know what was going to happen?"

He frowns. "No."

"I think you're lying. I think you had something to do with it."

He holds out his hands. "I didn't. I swear, you know?"

"Nicole's DNA was found in your front room. Her bike was seen at your house. You were seen talking to her on multiple occasions. You told us you didn't know her, but you lied."

He sits forward and rubs his hands on his trousers. He looks down at his shoes.

"Ed?"

He doesn't look up.

"Look at me, Ed."

He looks up, and tears are in his eyes.

"Do you have Nicole?"

He shakes his head.

"Do you know who does?"

He shakes his head.

"Why didn't you go to the performance? What did you know?"

"I couldn't," he says, barely a whisper.

"I can't hear you, Ed."

He sits up. "I couldn't."

"Why?"

"I'm not allowed. I can't go into a school, okay?"

He looks back down, and I glance over at Joyce, then back at him. I sit forward and point at the page in the file. "Your name isn't really Edward Warner, is it?"

He shakes his head without looking at me.

"Your name is Jacob Warner. You're a sex offender who didn't register your location when you moved here."

He looks up.

"Right?"

He nods.

"What did you do? How did you get on the list?"

He cups his hands over his nose and mouth. "I peed at a school playground."

I shake my head. "You didn't just pee. You did it on a slide while kids were at recess. Isn't that right, Ed?"

He moves his hands up to his forehead and looks down.

"That's really gross, Ed."

"I was just a kid too, you know? I was barely twenty and stuff and whatever. I was working at the construction site across the street, and some of the guys dared me. I wanted them to like me..." He takes his hands down and looks up. "I didn't know it would stay with me forever."

"Why didn't you register with the sheriff's office?" Joyce asks.

He looks up at her, pleading. "How could I? When people find out, nobody will hire me."

"Why did we find Nicole's DNA in your house, Ed?" I ask.

He turns to me and holds up a finger. "She came in once. Just once. I didn't want her to. She followed Domo. I couldn't stop her. She loved him. She just wanted to pet him and feed him."

"Domo, your dog?"

He nods. "I swear, I never touched her. She was such a sweet kid. She loved my dog."

I look at Joyce, and I know she sees the same thing I see. Ed's telling the truth. He doesn't have Nicole and doesn't know where she is.

"Who stole your sword, Ed?"

He shakes his head.

"Who?" Joyce shouts and slaps the table.

Ed jumps and swears he has no idea.

"No more lies," Joyce says, but Ed just shakes his head.

I sigh and look at Joyce. He's innocent. At least of this.

We both stand and walk to the door. I open it and wait for Joyce to exit, then turn back to him. "Ask for a lawyer. You're facing up to ten years in prison for not registering. You'd better get a good one if you don't want to spend a long time in here."

Chapter 32
Hank

It's late Friday night, technically Saturday morning, and I open Outlook and see I've received a new email from Trevor. It's also addressed to Joyce, and I wonder if she's seen it yet.

Detectives,

I finished my review of the security system installed at Skyline High School. I'm afraid it's not good news. The system sucks. There are holes in the surveillance area, and I can't see who broke into the cafeteria. I don't know if it's related to Nicole's disappearance. Sorry, I wish I could be of more help.

There is one thing I can tell you. Principal Skinner and Brenda Wallace had to know the camera in the front wasn't working. They've both logged into the system multiple times over the last week. I don't know why they didn't fix it. Maybe they didn't know how?

Let me know if you need anything else.

Trevor

I roll my chair back and lean out to ask Joyce her thoughts when I see the captain walking out of his office. He looks like he's done for the day. I'm surprised he's still here, but given everything going on and how many other people are here this late, I guess it makes sense.

He sees me and continues down the hall rather than turning toward the exit.

"Heads-up," I whisper. "Here comes the captain."

Joyce looks away from her computer and stands. I stay seated as Rigby approaches.

"What's the latest on the missing girl? Did you get anything from the handyman?"

"Not much," Joyce says. "I don't think he did it. We've searched his home and active job sites. His phone was on when Nicole was taken. He wasn't anywhere near the school."

He looks down and rubs his chin. "Do you have any other leads? I'm planning a press conference tomorrow morning. It would be nice to give them something."

"Nothing concrete. The camera equipment around the school wasn't any help. It didn't pick up anything unusual. One of the cameras was disconnected. We think whoever took her knew about the camera and its location."

"That means it has to be staff at the school, right? Who else would know?"

Joyce shakes her head. "Anyone with an internet browser. It's not hard to figure out that schools have cameras. You just need to know where to look."

He yawns. "Okay, well, text me the latest before eight tomorrow morning. If anything big breaks, call me."

He turns to walk away, but Joyce stops him.

"Sir?"

"Yeah."

"I'd like you to release Shawn Luelan. I think this disappearance shows us he's a victim rather than a killer. He didn't know what he was doing."

Rigby turns back to her. "I told you before, Joyce, solve the case and Shawn will be released. Until then, he stays where he is."

"There's a secret," Joyce says.

He frowns. "Huh?"

"Nicole. She was holding a secret. That's why she was taken. That's why Roy was killed. The kids in the class all knew a secret."

He puts his hand on top of the cubicle. "What secret?"

Joyce shakes her head. "We don't know. Shawn's father asked him about it today. Shawn said Nicole knew the secret but wouldn't say what it was. That's why she's gone. Someone is manipulating these kids. Leaving Shawn in jail is giving that person exactly what they want. They want the kids scared. They want to keep them quiet."

"So?"

"So let Shawn go home. Put an ankle monitor on him. Maybe then he'll open up and tell us what Nicole knew. Both their lives are at stake, not to mention the lives of Marilyn and Ty. We can't solve this case if you don't give us the tools to solve it."

The captain stares at her, then shakes his head. He turns and starts toward the exit, but Joyce follows. I get up from my chair and go after her, but she's already calling after him. Everyone in the building is watching the interaction now.

"You're a coward, Dale. What happened to you? How did you become this? An innocent kid is rotting in that jail cell, and you don't care."

He turns with fury in his eyes. "That's enough, Detective."

Joyce shakes her head. "No. That boy deserves to be at home with his father. If you aren't man enough to make it happen, we need someone who is."

Rigby looks around the room. His employees are watching him. He looks past Joyce at me. "Detective Gardner, take Detective Powers's gun from her." He turns and sees Ramirez and Coplan, another set of detectives. "Ramirez, Coplan, assist him in escorting Detective Powers from the headquarters. Collect her badge."

Ramirez and Coplan come forward and stand beside the captain. Coplan holds out his hand, and Joyce glares at him, then finally gives him her gun and badge. Ramirez reaches for her elbow, but she shrugs him off. She turns back and looks at me. The message is clear; she wants me to escort her out. I come forward and grip her elbow, ushering her out the back of the building to her car. She and I drove separately today. Normally, we don't when we have a case, but she was planning to leave work early to have dinner with Sam.

When we clear the door and are no longer visible to anyone inside, I release her, and we walk toward her car. She reaches the driver's side and turns back to me.

"What's wrong with you?" I ask. "This isn't you."

She looks up at me and shakes her head. "I just can't do it anymore. I can't stand by watching innocent people rot in jail. It's not right, and I had to take a stand. Besides, I was going to retire soon anyway. It's your time now."

She pats me on the shoulder, turns, and gets in the car. I step out of the way as she reverses, then stops. She rolls down her window. "Stick with the kids. Talk to Marilyn and Ty. One of them knows something. You're going to have to dig, but you can find it."

I nod, and she rolls up the window and exits the parking lot. I watch as her taillights fade behind my visible breath. After several seconds, I turn back to the building and see Captain Rigby standing by the doors. I wonder how much he's seen. He walks up to me and pats me on the shoulder. "It's your show now. Officer Levy is your new partner. Let's see how she does."

He continues over to his car and gets in. Within seconds, he's gone too.

I look up at the sky, the moon bright above, and listen to the silence. I don't know that I've ever felt more alone than I do at this moment. Not even when I left California and moved to Boise to play football. I knew nobody in Idaho then. But this feels worse. Joyce, my friend and partner, has deserted me. Not only that, she did it during perhaps the most challenging case of my career. As I look up at the moon, I can't see any stars. Just a giant white ball in the sky that looks as lonely as I feel.

Chapter 33

Sherry

I open my eyes and squint, trying to orient myself. It's dark, and I'm not in my bed. I hear my phone ringing, but it's not close to me. I sit up and remember. I fell asleep in Nicole's room, clutching her pillow. I get up and walk through my dark house, not turning on any lights. The phone stopped ringing before I could reach it. I pick it up and see I've missed multiple calls from the same number. A surge of anxiety grips me. Could it be someone who found Nicole? Is she...

I unlock the phone and hit redial.

After several seconds, a woman's voice comes on the line. "Mrs. Morgan?"

"Yes?" I say breathlessly.

"This is Janet, your mother's nurse in the hospital."

"Yes?" I say, feeling a fresh sense of fear.

"Ma'am, your mother is fading. If you'd like to say goodbye, you'd better get here soon."

"Okay, I'm coming. I'll be there in ten minutes."

I end the call and flip on the lights, blinking against the brightness. I'm not even sure what time it is as I stumble into my room and find a pair of leggings and a large hoodie. I put on a pair of tennis shoes and head down the stairs to my car. I open the garage and don't see my car. Then I remember. Nancy drove me home last night. My car is wrecked. I retreat into the house and remember Nancy gave me her car and keys.

I go back upstairs and try to remember where I put the keys. I was in Nicole's room. I go in and look around, then see a coloring book I pulled out last night. There's a blank page with a drawing Nicole made. It has two men standing on top of a house. Everything is drawn in black. I pick it up and stare at it for several seconds, then remember the keys and set it down.

I finally locate them in the pocket of the jeans I was wearing yesterday. I rush back down the stairs and run out the front door. It's dark, and the neighborhood is silent. Nancy's Mazda is sitting in the driveway. I notice with relief that, for the first time in days, it hasn't snowed overnight. I jump in the car, blowing on my hands, trying to warm my fingertips. I wish I had grabbed a pair of gloves. I start the car and look out the windshield. It's completely frosted. I turn up the defrost and consider trying to drive with the frosted glass but decide against it. The windshield is completely covered, and I just got in an accident because I was driving too fast in slippery conditions. I don't want to ruin Nancy's car as well.

I look around the inside of the vehicle, searching for a scraper but don't find one. Nancy always parks in the garage. When would she ever need one? I look down and realize I don't have my purse or phone. I groan and jump out of the car and run up the stairs and back into the house. I find my purse in my bedroom, then look through the kitchen and find a spatula. I run down the stairs and back out the door. I put my purse inside the car and notice the car has warmed a bit. I scrape the windshield, side windows, and back with the spatula, covering my hands with frost. Why didn't I grab gloves when I was in the house? I finish clearing the windows and jump back inside the car, smelling the heated air. My hands are so cold, they tingle and sting. I put the car in reverse and pull out of my driveway, reminding myself to slow down.

When I'm on the road, I take several deep breaths. I need to slow down and think. I look at the dashboard and see the time. It's six in the morning, and I'm pretty sure it's Saturday—no wonder the roads are empty. I pull the sleeves of the hoodie over my hands, thankful I don't have to touch the ice-cold steering wheel with my bare hands.

I reach the hospital and park in the lot in front of the main entrance. I know exactly where I'm going and ride the elevator to the second floor. When I reach my mother's room, Dr. Woodbury is standing by the bed holding a medical file. Janet, the nurse, stands beside her. They're looking at Mother and don't see me come in. I walk toward them, and they turn around. Dr. Woodbury reaches out and hugs me. It's a little strange; she's never hugged me before. She pulls back but keeps her hand on my shoulder.

"You can talk to her. It's hard to know how much she understands at this point, but I'm sure she'll enjoy hearing your voice."

I nod and look down at Mom. She's lying on her back, her face extended toward the ceiling, almost like she's reaching for air. Her breathing is loud and slow. Tears spring to my eyes, and I wonder how I could even have any tears left to cry. It feels like that's all I've done for the last few days.

"Mom," I say as I approach. "Mom, I'm here."

She doesn't move or respond. I look back at the doctor and the nurse. They've stepped back further, giving me room, their expressions grave. I turn back to Mom and reach for her hand. I hold it up to my lips and kiss it.

"Mom, it's Sherry. I'm here, Mom."

Her eyes don't open, but somehow I sense them react beneath her eyelids, and I feel her hand contract. She knows it's me. She's responding to me.

"Mom, you can go now. I'm going to be okay. I love you."

She squeezes my hand and holds it for several seconds, then I feel her fingers relax and go limp. I watch her closely, waiting for another breath, but it never comes. She was waiting for me. She wanted to say goodbye.

Chapter 34

Hank

I sit in the small conference room at police headquarters across the table from Officer Carol Levy. Last night, she became my partner after Captain Rigby suspended Joyce. I went home and tried to get a few hours of sleep, considering my next move. I decided to bring Levy up-to-date on the case, we've been sitting here for the last hour with me dumping information on her. Finally, she looks up from the file I put in front of her and leans back in her chair.

"So, who do you think is behind it? Who has Nicole?"

I shake my head and stand. "If I had to guess, I think it's one of the administrators in the school. Maybe a teacher or the principal. Joyce thinks the kids are the key. One of them has information we need." I turn toward the door. "I'm going to grab coffee. Do you want any?"

"No, I'm good."

I head out the door and walk down the hallway to the break room. I pour myself a cup of coffee, add some cream and sugar, then prepare to head back when Sarah pokes her head around the corner. She serves as our research assistant on cases.

"Hank?"

"Yeah."

"A woman is here. She wants to speak with you. I think she might be Mrs. Morgan."

I pause, holding the cup of coffee to my lips. "Okay, thanks, Sarah."

She disappears, and I walk out of the break room and down the hall. I reach the front and see Sherry Morgan seated in the lobby. She notices me and stands. She's wearing black leggings, a pair of white tennis shoes, and a large blue-and-orange Boise State hoodie.

"Hello, Mrs. Morgan," I say, holding out my hand.

She takes it. "Detective, can I talk to you?"

I consider taking her to the conference room but remember all the files and names written on the whiteboard. I change course and find an empty interview room and sit down opposite her on the other side of the table.

"What can I do for you?" I ask.

She's not wearing any makeup, and her hair is pulled back in a ponytail. Her eyes are puffy and red, which isn't a surprise given all she's dealing with.

"Is it true? Do you have Ed Warner in custody?"

I wonder who told her.

"Did he take my daughter?"

"No," I say and take a sip of coffee, watching her over the top.

"No? Then why did you arrest him?"

I consider how to answer. "He's being accused of something else."

"Something else? Like what?"

I scratch my chin. "Uh, well, he's required to register anytime he moves. He didn't."

She frowns, and the skin on her forehead crinkles. "Register? For what?"

I take another sip of the coffee. "He did something in his past, and because of it, he has certain restrictions."

The color drains from her face. "He's a sex offender."

I nod.

Her hand starts to tremble as she raises it to her cheek. "Did he do something to my daughter? She was seen with him. Her bike was at his house."

I extend my hand, trying to get her to pump the brakes on her assumptions. "We have no evidence he did anything to her. In fact, I think it's very unlikely he did."

"But you aren't sure."

I pause before shaking my head. "But I highly doubt it."

"How are you so sure he doesn't have her somewhere? Did you search his house?"

I nod. "We did. We've also searched his most recent construction jobs. We were also able to triangulate his location yesterday using his cell phone. He was never near the high school."

"You're sure?"

I shrug. "I can't say absolutely; there are ways to get around almost everything. But I'm confident he had nothing to do with her disappearance."

She puts her hands on her thighs and rubs them. "So, where are things now? Do you have any leads?"

I nod. "We've got a few things we're chasing down. Nothing concrete yet, but the day's still early. How's your mom?" I ask to deflect.

She looks down. "She died about an hour ago."

"Oh, I'm so sorry."

She clasps her hands in her lap and looks back up. "Thank you. She's the second family member I've lost this year. It doesn't get any easier."

I nod and look down at my cup. "Your husband?"

"Yes, which brings me to something I wanted to tell you."

"Oh?"

She folds her arms. "My husband died six months ago. His name was Ron. He was up on our roof, cleaning out a rain gutter, when he slipped off and fell onto the driveway. It caused a hemorrhage in his brain. He died the next day."

I watch her, marveling at how much she's been through over the last year and wondering how his death relates to Nicole.

"The last thing my mother said to me yesterday was that she believes Nicole did have a secret. And not only that, she said she thinks it's related to my husband's death."

I rub my jaw, considering that. "Okay. What do you think?"

She shakes her head. "I've been thinking about that all night. Nicole saw Ron die. She was out riding her bike when he fell from the roof. She was the closest to it. She was also the closest to Roy when Shawn stabbed him. She watched both deaths. Maybe they're somehow related. Maybe that's what her secret is about."

I nod. "So, you do think she has a secret?"

She shrugs. "I can't think of any other reason someone would take her."

I watch her but say nothing.

After several seconds, she says, "She's still alive, right?"

I look into her eyes and see that she needs me to tell her that everything will be okay. That Nicole will be fine, and we'll find her. But I know that's not something I can do. "I hope so. But I don't know for sure."

Her lip trembles, and she looks down. "I can't lose her, Detective. I just can't."

I want to distract her, change the subject, or talk about something else, but I need more information from her. As painful as it might be to talk about, I need to understand her and Nicole better. "She's your only child?"

She nods, still not looking up at me. "We tried for years to have children. Finally, when we'd given up, I got pregnant. I guess it works like that sometimes. She was our miracle child." She chuckles and wipes her tears. "She was such a beautiful baby. Everyone would always tell me so. Then, one day, when she was nine months old, I noticed she still wasn't awake late into the morning. She was sleeping in a crib by that time. I went in to wake her and couldn't. I called an ambulance, and the ambulance rushed her to the hospital. They did scans and found she had a tumor in her brain that created so much pressure it left her unconscious. They drilled a hole in her head, and the release of pressure caused her to wake up."

I hand her a box of tissues, and she wipes her nose and eyes.

"The complications from the surgeries caused her disability." She looks up at me. "Two years later, the tumors were back." She shakes her head and sighs. "I know I baby her. People tell me I shouldn't." She looks at me for understanding. "But wouldn't you? She's been through all that, then watched her father fall from a roof. I know I should have asked her for the secret. I know it seems like such a simple request on the outside, but I just couldn't. If we can't find her—" Her voice catches, and she stifles a sob. After several seconds, she wipes her eyes. "I should have asked her. I should have been more open with her."

I lean forward, putting a hand on her shoulder. "It's not your fault. We weren't even sure there was a secret. We still aren't."

She shrugs and looks down. "If we don't find her, I'll never forgive myself. I won't have anything else to live for."

She looks up into my eyes, and I ache for her.

"There's one other thing," she says.

"What's that?"

"Seymour Skinner grew up with my husband. I don't know if it's related, but they remained friends, even as adults. That's the only other link I can think of between Ron and Roy's accidents. Seymour is Nicole's principal. I don't think that's anything, but I thought I should mention it."

"Thank you. It probably isn't anything, but we'll check it out, just in case."

She stands, and I join her, opening the door and guiding her to the front of the building.

"Well, I'm going to go to the local church. My neighbor, Lisa Young, has organized a search. I'm going to go see what I can do. I have to keep busy."

I nod and extend my hand. She takes it and turns to leave, then stops. "Where's your partner? I was thinking I should apologize to her."

"She's off today."

"It wasn't because of what I said, was it?"

I shake my head.

"Will you let her know I'm sorry? I should never have talked to her that way. I realize now she was just doing her job. What you said about not wanting anyone else working on this case keeps rolling around in my head. It seems like we need her, don't we?"

I nod and watch her walk away. Just another reminder of how much I miss Joyce.

Chapter 35

Sherry

I can't believe the number of cars in the church parking lot as I turn into it and prepare to park. I look at the front doors and see Lisa waving to me. I don't know how she knew it was me. It's not even my car.

I find a space in the back of the lot, and before I can climb out, Lisa's beside the door. She extends her arms as I open it, and I step to her, letting her hold me for several seconds. She pulls back and looks at me.

"I'm so sorry about your mom."

"Thank you," I say.

"Come on, I want to show you what we're doing." She grips my hand and leads me to the doors. When we reach them, she stops and turns to me. "You don't have to, but maybe you could say a few words to the group of volunteers? They'd love to hear from you." She smiles and gives me an encouraging nod.

"Like what? What should I say?"

"Oh, nothing much. Just thank them for helping and maybe say something encouraging."

"Encouraging?"

"Yeah, like maybe you know that their efforts are going to bring Nicole home. Something like that. I just want to keep their spirits up, you know?"

She opens the church doors, and I think about the irony of her statement. She wants to keep *their* spirits up. She ushers me inside. I've never been a "believer" and can't remember the last time I've been inside a church. It's different from what I was expecting. More light and comfortable. There's furniture in the lobby and several paintings. She takes my arm and walks to the hallway as two young girls, I would guess early teens, come out of a door. They see us and retreat inside. I slow my steps, but Lisa guides me to the same door. She gives me a little squeeze and a wink, then opens the door.

The room is large with wood flooring and basketball standards on either end. There's a stage on one side. Several tables are set up throughout the room with chairs placed haphazardly. There must be at least a hundred people. Most are neighbors. Quite a few high school kids are here, including some I recognize. Lisa raises her arms and calls out for everyone to be quiet. Conversations stop, and all eyes turn to me.

"Thank you all for being here," Lisa says in a loud voice. "This is Sherry Morgan, Nicole's mother. She had something she wanted to say to you all."

Lisa turns and smiles again, hitting me with that encouraging nod.

I look out across the seemingly endless number of faces and see that many of them are recording with their cell phones. I wonder if this is being live streamed over the internet. I feel my body shaking, and my throat seizes. I cough to clear it and try to speak, but my voice comes out as a whisper. "Thank you all for coming." I see people frown and step closer. I clear my throat again and repeat myself, this time with a louder voice. "Thank you all for coming. It means so much to my family. I just know your efforts are going to bring," my voice catches, and tears spring to my eyes, "my daughter, Nicole...home."

Lisa wraps her arm around my shoulders and everyone claps. Several rush up, extending their arms and wrapping me in an embrace. I feel overwhelmed and lightheaded. The second person to hug me is Nancy. She holds me, then her husband. More neighbors come forward, embracing me as if we were long-lost friends. Half of the people in the room are high school kids. Most hang back, but a few come up and shake my hand and tell me how they know Nicole.

After fifteen minutes, Lisa grabs my hand and walks me over to a large chalkboard on wheels. There's a map of our town with color coding. She explains the areas they've already covered, knocking on doors and searching the surrounding areas. I see a picture of Nicole with the title "Missing" over the top and a phone number listed on the bottom. Lisa sees me eyeing it and tells me volunteers are spreading these photos around town.

I'm trying to keep up when I feel a gentle hand on my shoulder and turn around to see Mindy, the girl I asked to watch over Nicole. I'm surprised to see her. She wasn't here earlier. She's standing before me, tears running down her cheeks.

"I'm so sorry," she says.

Her tears make mine return, and I open my arms to her. We hug and cry.

"I let you down," she says into my shoulder. "You asked me to watch over her, and I failed you."

I pull back so I can look into her eyes. "No. We were late that day. It was my fault."

"I waited."

I put my hand on her cheek. "I know."

"I thought she wasn't coming. I had to get to class."

I shake my head. "It's not your fault."

She looks down. "Can I talk to you for a minute?" She motions to all the people standing around us. "Somewhere quieter?"

"Sure." I hold up a finger and try to find Lisa but can't. I see Nancy and tell her I'm leaving for a couple of minutes to talk with Mindy, and we sneak out the opposite door. We're on the other side from where I came in. I notice the classroom doors have windows in them, and I pick one that's empty and pull her in. We unfold a couple of the chairs and sit down so close that our knees touch.

"You know Ms. Thomas, the special ed teacher?" she says.

"Yes."

She looks up. "She knew this guy. This really weird guy." She holds a tissue in her hand and squeezes it.

"Weird how?"

"I don't really know how to describe him. He worked in construction."

"What's his name?"

"Ed, I think? I saw him only once or twice. I went with Ms. Thomas and a couple other kids to his house to pick up pieces of the set for the play. He was the one who built them."

"You went to his house?"

"Yeah, but not alone. There were a couple boys with us and Ms. Thomas."

"Okay. So what made him weird?"

She seems hesitant, like she doesn't want to tell me. "Do you know him? He lives right by your house."

I nod. "I've seen him a couple times. I haven't talked to him much."

She raises her finger and rubs it on her lips. "The thing is, I think something was going on between him and Ms. Thomas."

"What do you mean?"

She gives me a look like "you know."

"You mean she was dating him?"

Mindy nods.

"Are you sure?"

She shakes her head. "No, but you know how you just kind of get the feeling something is going on? That's how I felt. I think it was the way they looked at each other. I just keep thinking someone needs to check into him."

"You think he took Nicole?"

She shrugs. "Maybe he was helping someone."

We stare at each other, and I pick up her meaning. I reach forward and grasp her hand. "Thank you for telling me."

She nods. "I just want to be sure Nicole's safe."

Chapter 36
Hank

"What kind of music do you like?"

Officer Levy is looking at me, hand poised on the radio dial. It's a question Joyce never asked me. It didn't matter. She liked '80s and '90s rock, so that's what we listened to.

"If you had asked me that a year ago, I would have had a different answer."

She frowns. "How so?"

I shake my head. "Never mind." I wave a hand. "I don't care."

She nods and searches through stations and stops on 105.5. She leans back in the passenger seat, bobbing her head to the music. The song is a strange mix of country and rock. The guy uses a lot of electric guitar but sings about how his girlfriend kicked him out of the house, and now he's sleeping in his truck after getting drunk. I look at her out of the corner of my eye, then reach forward and hit one of the presets, changing the station. The new song is "Rock You Like a Hurricane" by the Scorpions.

"I thought you didn't care?" she says, raising an eyebrow.

"I guess I do."

We don't say anything else as we weave through the neighborhood, searching for the house. When we pull up, I'm not surprised by the size of it. Joyce and I investigated a case several months ago in this same neighborhood. Rita Burch lives just down the road.

When I shut off the car, Carol grabs my arm. "What am I supposed to do?"

"Investigate," I say.

"I know. But what does that mean, exactly?"

"You'll get the hang of it. Just follow my lead."

I get out of the car, and she joins me as we walk up to the front door. I ring the video doorbell and wait.

"Should I ask something?" Carol says.

I shrug. "If you want to."

The door opens, and a nice-looking woman in her early fifties stands in the doorframe. She's wearing a dark-blue USU sweatshirt.

"Detective Gardner?" she asks, holding out her hand.

I nod and take it. "Mrs. Sparrow, this is Officer Carol Levy."

They shake hands, and Mrs. Sparrow waves us in. She guides us to a sitting room next to the front door. There's a baby grand piano in one corner. She motions to a couch, then tells us she'll get Marilyn and walks away. We look around the room, admiring the furniture and artwork. After a couple of minutes, Marilyn comes down the stairs with her mother, trailed by a man. Marilyn and Mrs. Sparrow head for the other couch, but the man stops in front of me. I stand, and Levy joins me.

"Are you Hank Gardner?"

I nod.

He extends his hand. "Hal Sparrow. You played at Boise State, right?"

I nod again. Then motion to Levy and introduce them.

He walks to the chair closest to the piano. "Please, sit down," he says, sitting himself. "I thought I recognized your name when Angie said you called and wanted to talk with Marilyn. When did you give up football?"

"When nobody wanted to pay me to play anymore," I say and chuckle.

He laughs. "I remember you playing my Aggies. You seemed like you were in the backfield on every play. We couldn't block you."

"Sorry?" I say and he laughs.

"So, you're investigating Roy's death and Nicole's disappearance? I assume they're related." He looks at his wife. She's holding Marilyn's hand. "That's what they said on TV."

"Well, you can't believe everything you hear on TV. But, yes, we're operating as if there's a connection. Were you both there at the play that night?"

"Of course," he says, looking over at Marilyn. She's half seated beside her mother with her head on the couch pillow. She doesn't look at him. Her face registers both boredom and anger. "We were so excited to see our Mary perform. She did great."

Marilyn's eyes flick over to him, then go back to staring out into space.

"Did either of you notice anything unusual that night? Anything that seemed strange?"

Marilyn's parents look at each other, then shake their heads.

"Now that I think about it," Hal says, "I did notice a variation in the swords they were using. But I just thought that was because they were using whatever they could find. I didn't think one of them was an actual sword."

I nod, but before I can ask another question, Levy beats me to it.

"Did you think it was murder?"

I look at her, and Hal Sparrow frowns and seems confused. "What do you mean?"

"Did you think Shawn tried to kill the other boy?"

"I...I don't know. I think we were all in shock."

He looks at his wife and she nods.

This is the second time in less than ten minutes that I wish I had expressed my opinion to Levy more firmly. I look at her, then back at Hal Sparrow.

"Do you mind if I ask Marilyn a question?"

"Not at all."

I turn so I can look squarely at Marilyn. She's still got her face on the pillow, but her eyes are watching me.

"Marilyn, do you know about a secret?"

Her eyes move from me to her dad, and she sits up. She looks at her mom.

"It's okay, honey. Is there a secret at school?"

Her mom looks at me for confirmation and I nod.

"Nicole knows a secret," Marilyn says.

"Nicole does?" her mom says.

She nods. "Nicole knows lots of secrets. Ty knows too."

I sit forward on the couch. "Ty knows Nicole's secret?"

She nods. "He knows Nicole's favorite color."

"Is that the secret?" her mother asks.

"Ty knows her favorite color."

"What about any other secrets? Does Nicole have other secrets besides her favorite color?" I ask.

She nods. "Nicole knows lots of secrets."

"Do you know any other secrets?" her mother asks.

"Nicole has Oakridge Boys. Ty has Imagine Dragons. Ty likes dragons. Can I have some Oreos?"

Her mom smiles and looks at me. "She likes Oreos."

"Oreos are good," Marilyn says, looking away from her mom to me. "I like french fries." She focuses back on her mom. "Can we have french fries, Mom?"

Her mom laughs and rubs her shoulder. "Maybe in a few minutes. Can you tell us anything else about Nicole?"

She looks at her. "Ty likes Nicole. He likes to take her picture."

"He does? Does he have a camera?" her mom asks.

She shakes her head. "He has an iPad. He has lots of pictures of Nicole. He likes Imagine Dragons. He likes dragons."

"What about of you? Does he have pictures of you?"

She shrugs. "Maybe." She stands up from the couch and walks out of the room toward the kitchen.

"I'm sorry," her mom says, getting up and going after her.

"It's okay. We were done anyway."

We shake hands with her father, and he leads us out. When we get in the car, I see my phone is ringing. I answer and can't believe what I hear.

Chapter 37
Sherry

After entering the Bonneville County Jail and receiving directions, I check in with the guards and am ushered to a station in the lobby where I'm set up in front of a computer screen and given a pair of headphones. The guard who assists me looks at me curiously, and I know he recognizes either me or my name.

After less than a minute, Ed Warner comes on the screen. He's wearing a gray prisoner's uniform, and it's the first time I've seen him without a hat. I don't know why, but I'm surprised at how bald he is. I guess he just hid it well. We stare at each other for several seconds.

"Hello, Ed."

"Hey."

I've only talked to him briefly, but each time I struggle to understand him. He looks like a ventriloquist, barely opening his mouth when he speaks. His words are more grunts than actual words.

"Do you know why I'm here?"

"Nah."

"No idea, really?"

He shifts in his chair. "I didn't have nothin' to do with your daughter or whatever. I guess they ain't found her yet?"

"No, we haven't found her yet. Do you know where she is?"

"Nah."

"I've heard you were dating Georgette Thomas. Is that right?"

He swallows, and his eyes shift to the left.

"Is that true?"

"So what of it?"

"I understand you talked to my daughter, Nicole, more than once. I heard she even came into your house."

He shifts again in his chair.

"Is that true, Ed?"

Again, his eyes flash to the left, but this time he nods.

My voice becomes choked with emotion. "Did you ever touch my daughter?"

His eyes go wide. "Nah, never." He looks surprised by the question. "Nicole was a really nice girl and stuff. I never touched her. I swear it. She just liked my dog. You know?"

"Can I believe you, Ed?"

He nods, looking sincere. "Domo liked her too. She followed him into the house. She pet him and gave him treats, okay?"

I watch him.

"Cross my heart."

He makes the motion of drawing an *X* across his chest.

"Were you dating Nicole's teacher, Georgette Thomas?"

"We mighta gone to the Burly Burger a couple times."

"Did you ever talk about Nicole with her?"

He doesn't answer.

"Ed, what did she tell you about Nicole?"

"I don't know. She mighta said something about how Nicole was hard to handle in the school, you know?"

"Did she say anything else?"

He looks to the left again.

"Ed, what else did she say about Nicole?"

He leans forward and rubs his forehead. "She said the reason Nicole was like that, like a baby, was because you did it or whatever. You made her a baby." He brings his hands down. "I told her she was wrong, you know? I told her Nicole was sweet."

A thought occurs to me. "Ed, did you build the sets for the play because Georgette asked you to?"

A message on the screen says we only have two minutes left.

"Ed, do you think Georgette did anything to Nicole?"

He shakes his head.

"Ed, do you?"

"Nah, I don't think so."

"But you aren't sure?"

He hesitates.

"What, Ed? What is it?"

He swallows. "She said something one time, you know?"

"What did she say?"

"I don't think she meant it."

I look at the message, and it says we only have fifteen seconds.

"What, Ed?"

"She said that Nicole would be better off if—"

The screen goes black, and a message comes up telling me the session has ended. I slam my fists on the desk, and the guard rushes over.

"Sorry," I say, holding up my hands and backing away. "I didn't mean that."

He watches me, then points to the exit.

I leave the jail and rush to Nancy's car. When I get in, I start it, then dial Detective Gardner's number.

"Hello, Mrs. Morgan."

"Detective? You need to check on Georgette Thomas right now. I just met with Ed Warner in the jail. She was dating him. She got him to build the sets for the play. She told him Nicole would be better off without me. I think she has my daughter."

Chapter 38

Hank

Officer Levy and I sit in the car as I talk with Mrs. Morgan. When the conversation ends, I search for Sarah's number in my phone.

"What did she say?" Carol asks.

"She said Georgette Thomas and Ed Warner were dating and that Georgette had told him that Sherry Morgan was a bad mother. She wants us to talk to Ms. Thomas." I find Sarah's contact and call her.

"Hi, Hank," Sarah says on the other end of the line.

"Sarah, can you give me the address for Georgette Thomas?"

"Sure, one sec." I hear her typing. "Do you want me to text it?"

"Yeah, that would be great."

"Are you going over to talk to her right now?"

"Yes."

"Um, she might not be home. She's pretty active on social media. I saw her post something online about helping at the search head-quarters for Nicole."

"Really? How long ago was the post?"

Sarah types on her computer. "Less than an hour ago."

"Thanks. We'll go there first. Still, text me the address."

I put the car in gear and pull away from the curb.

"Was I okay in there?" Carol asks as I turn at a stop sign.

"Sure," I say.

She watches me. "I just...I felt like maybe I asked the wrong question."

I keep my eyes on the road, unsure of what to say.

"Did I?"

I look at her, then back to the road. "It wasn't a bad question. It was more about timing."

"What do you mean?"

I think back to when I was a brand-new detective and something Joyce had told me. "When you're talking to a witness or a person of interest, you want to structure your questions. Lead them to the information you need to know. Joyce gave me that advice. She told me to think about when you go to the gun range and shoot at a target. You want to group your shots. You don't want to shoot at all the targets, just one. And the better you get, the more focused the shots on that one target. Does that make sense?"

She nods.

"You want to purposefully place your shots. The same is true when you interview someone. Have an end in mind. Ask yourself what you're trying to achieve from the conversation, and focus your questions on your objective. Sometimes the answers people give might lead you astray, but always have a goal. As long as you do that, your questions will stay on point."

She nods and looks at the road. I can see she's digesting what I said.

We reach the church and get out of the car. A group of people stands by the front doors chatting in a semicircle. They don't react when we approach and pass them. As we walk down the hall toward the gym, I can hear footsteps behind us and look back to see that the group is following us. We enter the large room and find only six people inside. One of them is Lisa, the neighbor we saw at Ed's house. She sees us and comes over.

"Hi, can I help you?"

"Yes, we're looking for Georgette Thomas, Nicole's high school teacher. I heard she might be here."

"Oh, she was. She came for only a few minutes, though. She said there was something she had to do and left."

"How long ago was that?" I ask.

"Maybe twenty minutes."

"Did she say where she was going?"

She shakes her head. "Home, maybe? I don't know."

"Thank you."

We turn to leave, but she calls after us. "You're the detectives, right?"

I nod.

"Maybe you can give us an update on the case. It might help us know where to search for Nicole?"

I turn and look at her. My natural inclination is to think she wants some gossip, but as I look into her eyes, I get the feeling the question is genuine. I pull out my card and hand it to her.

"It looks like you're already doing all the right things. Just make sure to focus your efforts on places familiar to Nicole. Make sure people search with a buddy. Nobody alone. If you find anything, call me."

We walk out and get back in the car. Sarah texted the address, and Carol punches it into the GPS.

Ms. Thomas's house is only three minutes away. It's a small home, no bigger than a thousand square feet. The front of the house is simple, with a large maple tree in the middle of the yard. As we approach the door, I stop and look at Levy. I think about what Captain Rigby said when he assigned her to me. "Why don't you conduct the interview?" I say.

She looks at me, and her cheeks flush, or maybe it's just the nip in the air. "Me?"

"Sure."

"What should I say?"

I shrug. "You've interviewed suspects before. What do you want to learn from Ms. Thomas?"

She stares up at me, then looks at the front of the house. "If she took Nicole."

I nod and keep walking to the door. "Then focus your questions around that."

"Are you sure you want me to?"

I knock and step back. "Why not? I'll jump in if you need help."

She stands beside me and stiffens when the door opens. Georgette Thomas leans against the door, peering at us. I smile and wave, then look down at Levy.

"Georgette Thomas?" she asks.

"Yes."

"My name is Officer Levy, and this is Detective Gardner."

"I know who he is." She looks up at me through the screen. "Where's your partner?"

"Off today. Officer Levy is assisting me."

"Hmm," Georgette says.

"We're looking for Nicole Morgan and have some questions for you. Can we come in, ma'am?" Levy says.

Georgette sighs and pushes open the screen. We step in, and I move to the side so she can close the door behind me. She ushers us into her front room. It's small but tidy. She points to the couch, and we sit while she takes the chair opposite us.

"What do you want?" Georgette says.

I can't remember ever seeing the woman smile.

"We understand you went to the neighborhood search for Nicole today?"

"Yes."

She stares at Levy, almost as if she's challenging her.

Levy swallows. "Did you find out anything?"

Georgette glares at her, then looks at me. As much as I want to, I don't say anything and stare right back at her.

"Am I doing the investigating for you now?" she says with a sarcastic chuckle.

"Oh," Levy says and sits up a little straighter, "well, we were wondering when you were going to tell us you were dating Ed Warner."

Her eyebrows rise, and she looks caught off guard. "What business is it of yours?"

"As you know, we're trying to find Nicole, and Ed was seen with her on multiple occasions. He told us you had some not-so-nice things to say about her mother."

She chuckles. "Oh? And what exactly did I say?"

"You tell us," Levy fires back.

I fight to suppress a smile.

"What is this?" Georgette says, looking at me.

"Where were you on Friday at 7:40 a.m.?" Levy asks.

She looks back at her. "Teaching my class."

"Did you leave the school that day?"

"Not until after school was over. Long after, actually. You know. You saw me. We met in the office," she says, pointing to me.

"And you never left all day?" Levy asks.

"No?"

"Did you know Ed Warner was an unregistered sex offender?"

She shakes her head. "I didn't know he wasn't registered."

"But you knew he was a sex offender?" Levy asks.

Her spunk makes me smile.

"Yes, I did."

"Were you dating him?" Levy asks.

"We went on some dates."

"Did you bring him around your students?"

"Absolutely not."

"We understand some students went with you to his house to pick up set pieces for the play."

She pauses. "Yes, that's true."

"So, you did bring him around your students?" Levy says, her eyes blazing.

"I never brought him to the high school. That's what I meant to say."

"But you brought them to his house, knowingly endangering them. That's much worse."

"I beg your pardon," Georgette says, rising in her seat. "I never left them alone with him. They stayed outside with the truck while I went into the house. None of them were ever out of my sight. Besides, do you know why he's on the sex offender list?"

Levy looks unsure and I jump in. "He peed on a kid's playground toy."

"Exactly," Georgette says.

Levy looks at me, then sees I'm not going to speak. She turns back to Georgette. "Did you have anything to do with Nicole Morgan's disappearance?"

"Really?" she says, looking at me.

"Answer the question," Levy says.

"Of course not."

"Did Ed Warner?"

Georgette shakes her head.

"You're sure?"

"Yes."

Levy watches her, then looks at me.

"Do you have any ideas where she could be?" I ask.

Georgette shakes her head. "Don't you think if I did, I'd tell you?"

I nod and stand from the couch. "Thanks for your time."

Chapter 39

Sherry

After talking to Ed in the jail, I went back to the church and talked with Nancy and Lisa. They told me that a group of neighbors had planned a candlelight vigil for later that night. Realizing I hadn't yet showered for the day, they encouraged me to go home and fix myself up. At ten minutes to six, I drove to the high school and parked near the front. Nancy and Lisa were waiting for me and guided me to the front of the mass of people who had gathered there. Several TV trucks and vans littered the parking lot, and reporters spoke in front of cameras with bright lights.

When I reached the front, Lisa encouraged me to say something to the group of supporters. Knowing the cameras were rolling, I spoke to Nicole. I told her I loved her and couldn't wait to hug her again. After the brief speech, people crowded around me and embraced me. It was overwhelming, and at times, I didn't even know whose arms were around me. After twenty minutes, the crowd broke up, and people went back to their homes. Detective Gardner and his new partner watched from a distance.

Eventually, it was only me, my two friends, and their husbands remaining. Exhaustion overtook me, and I nearly passed out. Nancy's husband drove me home, while she followed in the car. He parked in the garage, and they came inside, forcing me to eat. Finally, I told them I would go to bed and they left.

That was four hours ago. I did fall asleep, but only for three hours. Now I've been awake, tossing and turning in my bed, thinking about Nicole and grieving my mother. I look up at the ceiling and think about my conversation with Ed. The detectives said they talked to Georgette but have their doubts about it being her. She was at the school all day. They verified that with multiple witnesses. There was no way she could have taken her. But the detectives admitted they had found a sword in Ed's house. It matched the one at the play that night. The one Shawn used to kill Roy. There has to be a connection between Ed and Nicole's disappearance.

I swing my legs out of the bed and get dressed in the leggings and hoodie I was wearing earlier. I put on a pair of boots and walk out the back door. I cross the snow-covered yard, my boots sinking into the snow. When I reach Ed's back door, I peer inside. The house is dark. I try the door handle and it turns. I push it open, and something brushes against my leg, almost knocking me over. I prepare to scream, then see it's Ed's dog, Domo. The dog runs out into the yard and does its business, then runs back to me, wagging its tail.

I'm not a dog person. Never have been. Nicole has repeatedly asked me for a dog, but I've always deflected, telling her that her father was allergic. Eventually, she stopped asking. The dog jumps up on my leg, and I pat its head, then walk into the house. The dog follows me, and I shut the door, feeling along the wall for a light switch. When I find one, I turn on the light.

I'm in the kitchen. The table is right in front of me, with four chairs. If I had walked any further, I would have run right into it. Domo watches me, then runs over to his bowl and water dish. Both are empty. He knocks them over with his nose, then looks at me. I take a step and hear a splash. I look down and see I'm standing in a puddle of urine. The dog had been left here alone for at least a day. Considering the puddle is beside the back door, I'd say he did his best to hold out as long as he could.

I take a long step, avoiding any more splashes, and search in the cupboards and drawers, looking for dog food. I finally find it in the pantry and pour it into the bowl. Domo wags his little tail and chomps on the food. I pick up his water bowl and fill it in the sink, then place it next to the food. He leaves the food bowl and begins lapping up the water, spilling it on the wood floor. I grab a paper towel and wipe up the urine puddle, along with another present he left close by.

Not caring how cold it is, I open the back door, letting fresh air fill the kitchen. Within a few seconds, I can already tell the smell is improving. I sit down at the kitchen table and watch Domo. After a couple minutes, he finishes eating and drinking and comes over to me. He jumps up on my leg, and I pat his head. He tries to lick my hand, but I'm not having it and raise my hands and put them on the table. He gives up and lies down at my feet.

After several seconds, I stand and begin exploring the house. I start with the upstairs, going into Ed's bedroom and looking around. I don't know what I'm looking for, I'm just looking. I cross the hall and find another bedroom. It's been converted into an office with a desk and an ancient desktop computer. I look through some papers on the desk, then exit and walk down the hall. I find steps leading to the basement and turn on the lights before descending. I open all the doors, most of them closets or storage. I see a spot on the wall where something used to hang, and I imagine that's where the swords were kept.

I stare at the space, thinking. If Ed didn't bring the sword to the play, who did? Someone who knew it was there. If they knew Ed well enough to know he had swords in his basement, then they must also know what he does for work. I remember him telling me most of his jobs were for investment properties. Investors would buy a place and hire him to go fix it up before selling. Those places would be empty. Wouldn't that be the perfect place to hide a kidnapped child like Nicole?

I go back upstairs and rummage through Ed's desk. He has receipts from various hardware stores and several past-due tax letters. While looking through them, I bump the computer mouse on the desk, and the monitor lights up. The computer is running an outdated version of Windows and has QuickBooks open. There's an invoice with a name and address that Ed created. The invoice has a date. It was earlier this week. I find a pen and paper and write the address. I notice the Next button is grayed out, so I press Previous instead.

It's another invoice. This time, the date is two days earlier. I note this address as well. I continue until I have his last ten addresses written on the sheet of paper. I look at the time on the computer and see it's past 1:00 a.m. Domo followed me into the room and trails me as I walk down the hall to the kitchen and the back door. I turn out the lights and wave goodbye to him as I exit the house. I cross the yard, reenter my home, and search for my phone. I don't even look at it and put it in my pocket, then go to the garage and get in Nancy's car. I open the garage and pull out of the driveway.

Although I feel exhausted, I know I won't sleep tonight unless I check some of these addresses. I look at the sheet and recognize where the first house is. I grew up on that road. It's only ten minutes from here. I drive with the radio off, lost in thought. I reach the house and turn off my headlights, parking beside the curb. It's dark inside and out. The only light comes from a streetlamp across the road. I look around at the snow surrounding the house and see none of it has been disturbed. There's no way someone entered this house without a helicopter, unless...

I get out of the car and walk to the wooden fence surrounding the back of the house. I peer through the gaps in the wood, looking for any sign of activity. There's nothing. I walk across the front of the house to the other side of the fence. This side has a gate but it's locked. Again, I peer through the wooden slats, searching for footprints. Again, I find none.

I get back in the car and look at my list. I don't recognize the second one, pull out my phone to use the GPS, and push the side button, but it doesn't light up. The phone is dead. I search Nancy's car, looking for a charger but can't find one. I guess my only option is to go home. I look at the list one more time and see an address I recognize. At least, it's a street I'm familiar with. I had a high school friend who lived there.

I decide to go there rather than home. It's only five minutes away, and with no traffic in the middle of the night, I get there with ease. When I pull up to the house, I see it's only four houses from my friend's childhood home. It's also dark, just like the previous house. Again, I search the snow surrounding the home, but this time I see footprints. But the footprints aren't on the driveway. They're on the side of the house, leading to the fence gate.

I get out of the car and walk over to examine the footprints. There are a lot of prints, but as I analyze them, I recognize that only some lead to the house. Others lead away. The prints that lead away are the same prints. The same person has been going in and out of the home. Maybe Ed? I bend down and look closer at the other set of prints. There's only one set of those, and they only lead toward the house. Never out. The prints are small. Child size. They could be Nicole's.

I follow the prints up to the gate and try to open it, but it's locked. I look around, searching for anything I can use to climb the fence. Not finding anything, I go to the front of the house and try the door. It's locked. The windows have shades that are drawn, and I can't see inside. I return to the fence and find I can get traction on the brick wall of the house beside the fence. I place my hands on the top, press my body against the brick, and leverage myself up. I reach the top and can't figure out what to do next. I turn into the fence, and my momentum pushes me forward. Unable to stop it, I fall and crash onto my back in the snow. I gasp for breath, snow covering my face. I try to breathe but can't. The wind has been knocked out of me. I raise my knees and stare at the dark sky, praying for air.

Finally, my body allows a quick breath, and I'm gasping now.

I lay that way for a minute or two, regaining my breath. Eventually, I roll to my side and stand. I feel a jolt of pain in my back and crouch forward. My fingers are almost numb, and my hoodie is covered with fresh powder. I go to my knees, then stand and brush myself off. I look around and find the footprints and follow them to the back of the house. This is the last one, I tell myself as I take slow steps. I can't do any more tonight. There's a walkout basement, and the footprints lead to it. I approach the door and stop before grasping the handle. I take a breath and grip it. It turns, and the door opens.

I hear a faint beep as I step into the room. It's dark, but my eyes adjust quickly, and I see it's mostly empty. There's a small kitchen with a fridge, oven, and counter. There's no furniture other than a couple chairs at the bar. I close the door behind me and open the fridge. There's food inside. I close it and retreat to the door. Someone lives here. I've broken into someone's house. I grip the door handle, ready to open the door, when I stop and think. I turn back, letting my eyes readjust to the light. I should leave, right? I should call Detective Gardner and have the police come. I know I should but I don't.

On the other side of the room, I can make out several doors, and I walk to them, opening them. The first is a closet, but the second is a bedroom, and it's occupied. A person is sleeping on an air mattress lying on the floor. I jerk back, but then notice the body is small. I'm not sure, but I think I recognize the shape. I take a step toward the body lying in the bed when I feel something hard pressed against the back of my head. I jerk to the side and try to turn around when I hear the click of a gun hammer.

Chapter 40
Hank

"How did I do yesterday?" Carol asks from the passenger seat.

It's been forty-eight hours since Nicole's abduction, and we're driving to Ty Malone's house. It's Sunday morning, and the town feels peaceful. Nobody would guess the turmoil it's seen over the last several days.

"You did great," I say, pulling up to the house.

"Yeah?" She smiles, and her eyes sparkle like a kid being given a trophy. "Any pointers for today?"

I shrug. "Same aim as Marilyn. Let's try to find out if Ty knows the secret. I'm also curious whether he saw anything when Roy was killed. If you remember, Principal Skinner said he was handling the lights on the stage when the accident happened. Ty left for the bathroom. Maybe that's significant. Maybe he saw something."

We get out of the car and approach the house. Before we knock, the door opens, and Ty stands in the doorway. We called his mother to warn her we were coming. Looks like she told Ty, and he's eager to talk. A rarity in our line of work.

"Hey, I know you," Ty says, pointing at me. "You were at my school."

Ty's mother stands behind him and smiles, holding him back. He's a friendly kid and seems to welcome visitors.

"How are you, Ty?" I say as we step into the house. I extend my hand to him, and he grasps it.

"Wow. Your hand is big!" He turns it over so he can look more closely. "Your skin is dark like chocolate."

I chuckle, and Ty's mom apologizes and pulls him back.

Officer Levy shakes his hand, and they lead us into their TV room beside the kitchen. The couch is a sectional, and we sit on one side while Ty and his mom sit on the other. Ty scoots closer to us, and his mom scolds him and pulls him back, keeping a hand around his bicep.

"What's your name?" Ty asks Officer Levy.

"Carol."

"Carol," he repeats, then looks at me. "What's your name?"

"Hank."

"Hank," he says, then repeats it several times. "I'm Ty." He points to himself. "My dad's at work. He works at the hospital. His name is Jim. Do you know him?"

We shake our heads.

"He's a good dad." He turns and looks at his mom, and she smiles and nods. "This is my mom. Her name's Rhonda. She's a good mom." He pats her knee.

His mom smiles. "Ty, these people are detectives. They have some questions for you. Can you let them ask their questions?"

He looks at her and nods.

"Ty," Carol says. "We heard Nicole, from your class in school, knows a secret. Do you know what the secret is?"

He nods. "Nicole has a secret."

"She does? What is the secret?"

He looks at her, then at his mom. "Nicole knows the secret."

His mom puts her hand on his shoulder. "I know. Do you know what the secret is?"

He shakes his head. "It's Nicole's secret. I took a picture on my iPad, and Nicole said it was a secret."

Levy and I sit forward, and Ty's mom looks at us, then back at her son.

"Ty, honey, why don't you go get your iPad? You can show us the pictures on it."

"Okay, Mom," Ty says and walks to the stairs. He turns back around. "My iPad is in my room charging. It was out of batteries."

"Okay, honey. Go get it. Bring the charger."

"Mom, you said to let it charge."

She smiles. "This time, it's okay to not let it charge all the way. Go get it."

He looks confused but turns and goes up the stairs anyway.

His mom looks at us. "Do you know who took Nicole?"

I shake my head. "We've been tracking some leads but nothing concrete. Maybe this is the break we need."

Ty comes down the stairs with the iPad and sits beside his mom. We crowd around him as he unlocks it and goes to the photo app. He clicks on the most recent. It's a photo of the TV with a man holding a microphone.

"Do you like Imagine Dragons?" he says to Carol.

"I do."

"What's your favorite song?"

"Hmm, I like all of them."

He nods and shakes with excitement. "Me too! I love them all too. My favorite is 'Radioactive.'" He bobs his head and pretends to play an air guitar while sounding the instruments with his voice. "They're from Idaho, like me."

"I know," Carol says.

For the next fifteen minutes, Ty flips through his pictures one by one, explaining each. There are many random shots of the school and people in it but nothing that seems unusual. Certainly nothing to keep secret.

"Ty, can I hold your iPad for a minute?" I ask.

He looks at me warily and pulls back.

"I promise I won't do anything to harm it. I just want to check something. I'll stay right here with it."

He looks at his mom, and she gives him an encouraging nod. Reluctantly, he hands it over, then forces Carol to exchange seats with him so he can be right beside it.

I open the albums portion of the photo app and go to recently deleted. There are six photos in that section. I click on the first to make it larger and see something that we've been looking for.

"That's it!" Ty exclaims. "That's the one Nicole said is a secret."

Chapter 41

Hank

We pull up in front of the house, and I look over at Carol. She hasn't spoken since we left Ty's place. She grips her knees and looks at me. I can see the anxiety on her face.

"Will you take the lead on this one?"

I nod. I was planning on it.

"Shall we?" I ask.

She nods, and we get out of the car and approach the house. There's a car parked in the driveway, and I hear music coming from the speakers. I see a young man, early twenties, sitting behind the wheel. He sees us and startles. I wave and continue to the front door. We ring the bell, and I shoot Carol an encouraging smile. The door opens, and a woman gives us a curious look.

"Is Seymour Skinner here?" I ask.

She nods. "Who may I ask is calling?"

"My name is Detective Gardner, and this is Officer Levy of the Idaho Falls Police Department. He'll know us."

"You can come in."

We step inside, and she tells us she'll get him.

The house is warm and comfortable. It's not a big house, but it's beautifully furnished and decorated. On the wall beside the staircase are four large framed pictures. Two feature married couples on their wedding days. The other two are single photos of a boy and a girl. The last one is the boy sitting out front in his car.

Principal Skinner appears at the top of the stairs, followed by his wife. He comes down, and I see anxiety on his face. I wonder if he's been expecting us.

"Detectives," he says in an exaggeratedly joyous tone. "So good to see you." He holds out his hand, and I shake it. He leads us into the kitchen, and we sit around the table. "Did something happen? Is there something new I can help you with?"

His wife walks to the food-preparation area and begins washing dishes.

"Principal, what we're about to say might be best in a private setting. If you'd like, we can take you down to the police station to have this discussion."

His cheeks turn red, and his wife stops the water and stares at us with a dish in her hand. He turns, looks at her, then turns back.

"No, go ahead. We can talk here."

"Are you sure?"

He nods, and I take out my phone and pull up the image from Ty's iPad. I hold it out so he can see it. He looks at it for several seconds, then looks down at his hands. His wife leaned over the counter when I showed him, but I don't think she could see much from her angle.

"Where did you get that photo?" Skinner asks, swallowing.

"A student had it and several others," I say. I glance at Carol, then at Skinner's wife. "Have you been engaged in a sexual relationship with that student?"

His wife drops the dish into the sink and looks down. Skinner turns back to her, and when he speaks, it isn't to me. "Yes," he says.

His wife gasps and raises her hands to cover her face. Skinner stares at her for several seconds, her eyes not meeting his, then turns forward and looks at his hands on the table.

"How long?" I ask.

"Almost a year."

His wife sobs and puts her hand over her mouth.

When we walked in, I wasn't sure what type of crime had been committed. Now, hearing when the relationship began and the age of the girl, some of those questions have been answered.

"Do you know where she is now?"

He shakes his head. "I've been trying to reach her since Friday. She won't answer my calls or texts. I don't know, but I worry that she might have Nicole."

I nod. "Do you have any idea where she might have taken her?"

He shakes his head.

"Was it you or her who placed the sword on the stage for Shawn to use during the play?"

He looks up at me. "It wasn't me. I was as shocked as everyone else when Shawn stabbed Roy. I'd been planning to confess the relationship the next day. I had an appointment set with the superintendent. But then, when that happened...I don't know. I got scared."

"Did the girl know you were going to confess?"

He nods. "I told her about Roy."

"What about him?"

"Roy came to my office. He told me he knew I was doing something bad with a girl in the school."

"That's how he said it? Something bad?"

"Yes."

"What did you say?"

"At first, I denied it. I thought I could convince him that he was wrong. But he wasn't having it."

"What then?"

"I convinced him to let me confess after the play."

"How did Roy find out?"

"He saw us in a," he pauses and tilts his head, "compromised position." He turns, looking at his wife. Her head is down. She's not looking at him. He turns back to us. "I knew I had no choice. Roy was going to expose us. The girl begged me not to confess, but I told her I had to."

"But you didn't confess after Roy was killed."

He looks at me, then drops his head.

"Do you know how she got the sword?"

He shrugs. "After that, I couldn't control her. She wouldn't listen to me."

I nod and motion to Carol. We stand, and Carol tells him he's under arrest. She reads him his Miranda rights, then asks him to stand and turn around. He does, and Carol cuffs his arms behind his back, then guides him out when his wife finally speaks.

"Stop," she says and looks up. Her cheeks are red, fire in her eyes. She opens the drawer next to her, and I can see her actions before she does them. I step over to her and stop her before she can pull the knife from the drawer. She looks up at me, and I shake my head, holding her wrists. Her face crumples, and tears well up. She stops fighting to get loose from my grip, and I allow her to raise her hands and cover her face. She turns and runs from the room, and I motion to Levy, and she guides Skinner to the front door. When we reach it, the door opens, and his son enters, looking at us in surprise. He sees Carol's hand on his father's shoulder, then notices the handcuffs.

"Dad? What's going on?"

Skinner doesn't even look at him; instead, he pushes forward, exiting his house.

Chapter 42
Sherry

The room I'm being kept in is completely dark. No windows or light of any kind. I'm in the house's basement in a storage closet. After finding Nicole, a gun was placed against the side of my head, and I was led into this room. I was forced to the ground as duct tape was wrapped around my ankles and wrists and over my mouth.

"You should have left us alone," Mindy had whispered before closing the door.

I've been sitting in the same position for hours, my back leaning against a cement wall.

"You're awake," Mindy says beyond the closed door. The light in the other room flicks on, and a faint glow peeks through the gap in the bottom of the door.

"Yep," Nicole says.

"Did you sleep okay?"

If Nicole responds, it's too soft for me to hear.

"Come over here to the counter," Mindy says. "I'll get you cereal."

I hear what sounds like a chair moving, then feet shuffling, and a milk jug being dropped onto a counter. Cereal is poured from the box into a bowl.

"Can I see my mom today?" Nicole asks.

More cereal is poured into the bowl, then the fridge opens and closes before a chair is moved.

"I have something really sad to tell you," Mindy says. "Your mom was in a car accident. Your grandma too."

Nicole doesn't respond.

After several seconds: "They both died in the accident. I'm so sorry, Nicole."

They're quiet for minutes; the only sound is the light crunching of cereal.

I'm in agony. My daughter, my baby, is in the other room being told I'm dead. The tape around my wrists, ankles, and mouth is too tight. Even when I try to scream, it only comes out muffled.

I hear feet shuffling, then Mindy asks Nicole if she wants more. Nicole says no, and the refrigerator opens.

"Can I color?" Nicole asks.

"Of course."

I hear her footsteps, but then they stop close to my door.

"I know you're upset, but Idaho isn't safe anymore. That's why we need to leave. We're going away tonight."

Chapter 43

Hank

When we pull up in front of Mindy's house, I look around, searching for her car, the old Ford Escort with more rust than paint. But I don't see it. We get out of our car and approach the house. I knock on the door and nobody answers. I knock again and ask Carol to call Mindy's mother. She gets out her phone and starts dialing the number when the door opens. The woman is younger than I would have expected. She can't be forty yet, and she has the same long, beautiful hair and eyelashes.

"Mrs. Decker?" I ask.

"No," she says and starts to close the door.

"We're looking for Mindy Decker's mother. Is that you?"

She stops and peers at us more closely. "What of it?"

I hold out my badge. "Ma'am, my name is Detective Hank Gardner, and this is Officer Carol Levy. We'd like to speak to your daughter. Is she home?"

She frowns and shakes her head. "She's staying at a girlfriend's house this weekend."

I nod. "It's really important that we find her. Which girlfriend is she staying with?"

Mindy's mom glares at me. "What's going on? Why do you want to talk to Mindy?"

"Ma'am, we believe Mindy might be able to help us with our investigation. We'd like to talk to her. What's the name of the girl she's staying with?"

"I don't know. Kayla."

"Kayla? Great. Do you know her last name?"

She puts her fingers to her lips and looks up. "Kayla...Kayla...Anderson, maybe?"

"Good." I look over at Levy, but she's already noting the name. "Ma'am, can you tell us the last time you saw your daughter?"

She peers at me. "What did she do? What's going on?"

I can see this time I'm not going to be able to evade her question, but I also don't want her to know the real reason we're looking for her.

"Have you heard there's a girl from her high school, Nicole Morgan, who's missing?"

She nods.

"We think Mindy might have been one of the last people to see her at the school. She might be able to help provide information."

"Oh. I don't know. Maybe Thursday night, I guess."

"You didn't see her Friday morning?"

"I work late on Thursdays. I wasn't up yet when she left for school."

I nod. "Have you talked to her at all this weekend?"

She shakes her head. "You know how teenagers are; if you aren't giving them money or food, they aren't interested in talking to you."

I nod. "Isn't that the truth? Would you mind calling her?"

"Sure. Let me get my phone. Hold on."

She walks away but doesn't invite us in. We remain on the porch looking at each other. After several seconds, Mindy's mom returns with the phone pressed to her ear. After only a few seconds, she shakes her head and hangs up. "Nothing. Straight to voicemail. I could text her?"

"Okay. But maybe don't tell her we want to talk to her. Teenagers sometimes get freaked out by the cops, thinking they're in trouble. Maybe just tell her to call you." I reach out and hand her my card. "If you hear from her, find out where she is and call me immediately. That would be a big help."

We get back in the car, and I look at Carol.

"What do you want to do?" she asks.

I look back and see Mindy's mom watching us from the window. "Let's get a car here to watch the house. Make sure it's plain. Do the same with Kayla's place."

"I'm on it," Carol says and pulls out her phone.

"Also, put a BOLO on a '95 green or blue Ford Escort. Have them look up the plates."

Carol nods, and I sit and think while she talks on the phone. If I were a high school girl with little money, where would I hide? Where would I go?

I get an idea and start the car. I drive several blocks, and we pull up in front of Ed Warner's house. Carol hangs up and gives me a curious look. I get out of the car, and she follows me into the house. When we open the door, Domo, the dog, barks and comes running toward us. His tail is wagging, and he jumps up on my leg. I pat his head and look around. Why hasn't Animal Services come to get the dog? We called it in.

I walk down the hall toward Ed's office and notice several drawers are open in the desk. Someone has been here. I move the computer's mouse, and the screen comes on. A software program is open with an invoice for a customer. I get up from the desk and walk back down the hall.

"What is it?" Carol asks as she follows me.

I walk into the kitchen and look around. Domo sits beside the back door. When I walk over and let him out, I notice footprints in the snow. I walk out the back door and follow them. They lead to the neighbor's house behind Ed's. It's Sherry's place. I reach her back door and knock. Nobody answers. I try the door and it opens.

"Sherry?" I call, standing at the door. "Sherry? Are you here?"

The house is silent. I pull out my phone and dial her number. The call goes to voicemail.

"Where is she?" Carol asks.

I shake my head and walk into the house. We search room to room. On Nicole's bed, I find a picture of two stick figures standing on top of a house. Nicole drew it. Everything is black, even the trees. There's something about it that draws my attention, and I fold it up and put it in my pocket. I return to the kitchen and find Carol there. I dial the number of Lisa Young, the neighbor who organized the search for Nicole.

When she answers, I say, "Mrs. Young, this is Detective Gardner. Have you seen Sherry Morgan today?"

"Hi, Detective. No, I tried calling her, but her phone goes straight to voicemail. Is she okay?"

I ignore the question. "If you talk to her, will you let her know I need to speak with her?"

"Did something happen? Did you find Nicole?"

"No. But I have a question I need to ask her. Thank you."

I end the call before she can ask anything else. I look at Carol, and we walk out of the house and across the backyard. We reenter Ed's house, and I return to his office. When I sit down at the desk, I look at Carol. "Will you check the rest of the house? See if you can spot anything that Sherry might have been looking at."

She nods, and I look at the computer screen. Why would she be looking at a customer invoice? Then it hits me. Ed fixes vacant houses. Mindy has no money for a hotel or anything else. If she took Nicole, she could stash her in one of those houses. If Mindy took the sword and placed it on the stage, she knew Ed.

I open my notes app on my phone and look at the computer. There's a Previous button on the screen. I note the address of the invoice on the screen, then go back all the way to the most recent. It's a list of ten addresses. Nicole, and now maybe Sherry, are being held in one of those houses. But for how long? Mindy has killed before, and I have no doubt she'll kill again.

Chapter 44

Sherry

"Do you want to watch Sesee?" I hear Mindy ask Nicole from behind the locked door.

Nicole says she does.

"Come on. You can watch it upstairs on my iPad. I've got headphones for you."

I hear footsteps, then a door opening and closing, then creaks on the stairs. After several seconds, I hear their footsteps directly above me. After a few more seconds, only silence. I shift my weight from one side to the other. I've been sitting on the cold concrete floor for hours with my ankles, wrists, and mouth bound with duct tape. My sit bones are aching, and I stretch out my legs and arms, trying to get some blood flow, when I hear footsteps above me. They're on the steps now, descending to my level. The door to the stairs opens and closes, and within seconds, I hear a click in the lock of my door, and it swings open. The light flips on, and I have to blink against it. Mindy closes the door and comes forward, peering at me.

"I really wish you hadn't come, Mrs. Morgan. I planned to keep you out of this whole thing." She sits on the floor opposite me and crosses her legs. "Are you thirsty?" Her tone is sweet, almost kind.

I nod and try to respond, but it comes out as a mumble.

She holds up a water bottle and shows it to me. "I want to help you. I don't want you to suffer. I'll give you some of this water if you promise to answer my questions. Okay?"

I nod, and she comes forward. She grips the side of the tape placed over my mouth and pauses, looking at me. "This is going to hurt." She rips the tape from my face.

I cry out. Searing heat covers my mouth, chin, and cheeks.

"Sorry about that," she says with a look of concern.

I take a deep breath and scream as loud as I can. Mindy slaps me across the face. I careen to the side, feeling the sting of the slap, and I look back at her.

"I trusted you," she says, scowling. She obviously misses the irony of the statement. She stands and grabs the roll of duct tape.

"Wait," I say, holding up my bound hands. "I won't do that again. I promise."

She looks at me, measures out a piece of tape, then bites the edge, ripping off a piece. She holds it between her hands and extends it toward my mouth.

I lean back, turning away. "I promise. I won't scream again."

She stops and stares into my eyes. She watches me for several seconds, then sits back in her cross-legged style. "Prove it. Answer a few questions, then I'll give you some water."

"Okay."

"Who else knows you're here?"

"Nobody."

"Nobody?" she says with skepticism.

"I swear."

"How did you find us? How did you know we were here?"

"Can I have some water?"

She shakes her head. "Answer my question."

"I went and talked to Ed Warner at the jail. He told me he supplied the set for the play and the swords. He said it was his sword that killed Roy. I figured that whoever stole his sword must have known him pretty well. I went to his house and looked at his computer and found the jobs he's worked on. I didn't know for sure, but I thought these houses were empty and might be a good place to stay hidden." I shake my head. "I didn't know it was you."

"Hmm." She leans forward, holding the water bottle to my lips. She pours it slowly, but some of it still runs down my chin to my chest. After several gulps, she pulls back and resumes her position. "Pretty clever, Mrs. Morgan."

We stare at each other for several seconds.

"Well," she says, holding up my cell phone, "lucky for me and for you, your cell phone was dead when you got here. Otherwise, I'd have had to kill you and run before we were ready."

"Ready?" I ask.

She nods. "We're leaving Idaho Falls." She shrugs. "Leaving Idaho, actually."

"Where are you going?"

She smiles. "If I tell you, I'll have to kill you." She grimaces. "Do you want that?"

I grunt. "You're going to kill me anyway."

She nods. "Probably."

I can't believe how nonchalant she is about it.

"Why are you doing this?" I ask.

She shrugs. "Love."

"Love?"

She nods.

"Love of who?"

"Seymour."

"Skinner?"

She nods. "We've been lovers for more than a year now. I love him, and he loves me. Do you know how lucky I am to have found my soulmate? To have him be my principal?"

I stare at her, not comprehending. "Mindy, that's not love. He seduced you. He took advantage of a young girl."

She grins and laughs. "Other way around, I'm afraid."

My mouth drops open. "What do you mean? He could be your father!"

She chuckles. "I know...isn't that hot?" She laughs at my expression. "So? I like it. I like older men. The boys my age are so juvenile and stupid." She gets a wistful look in her eyes. "He's...mature. From the first time I saw him, I yearned for him. Have you ever felt that? Has a man ever done that to you?"

I don't answer.

She smiles at the memory. "At first, he hardly noticed me. I liked to flirt with him, try to get his attention. He wouldn't respond, even though I could see in his eyes that he liked it."

"How could you tell?"

She chuckles. "Because of the way he watched me." She shakes her head. "Oh, don't think it was only me. I wasn't the only one he watched. He liked some of the other girls too. But I could see he was especially fond of me. But he never acted on it. He was always such a good boy. Finally, one day, I decided to take control."

I can't believe what I'm hearing. "How?"

She winks. "By giving him what he wanted." She places her finger on the front of her blouse and pulls it down to reveal cleavage. "I gave him more to see."

I frown. "You changed your dress?"

She laughs. "Aren't you innocent? How did you manage to make a baby?" She shakes her head. "Not just that. I put a note on his desk with a picture. You can figure out what happened after that."

I shake my head. "Mindy, this isn't going to work. He's married. He's the principal. If people find out..."

Her eyes go wide. "What? People will be shocked?" She throws up her hands. "Scandal in little old Idaho Falls? So what? That'll just put us together sooner. He can leave his stupid, fat, ugly wife and be with me."

"Does he know you're here?"

She shakes her head.

"He knows you took Nicole?"

"Probably."

"Why? Why take Nicole?"

She shakes her head. "That was never the plan. I didn't want to. I had to. She forced me."

"Forced you? How?"

"Nicole knew too much. She's known for a while, and it hasn't been an issue. But that changed on Thursday. It forced me to act."

"What happened on Thursday?"

She smiles.

"She saw you with Seymour?"

She shakes her head.

"What then?"

"She told me about your husband."

I frown and feel like I might gag. "My husband? What about him? You didn't..."

She shakes her head. "Of course not. But he saw us together."

"You and Seymour? When?"

"The day before he died. Before his accident."

Tears come to my eyes, and rage bursts within me. "Did you do it? Did you do something to make him fall? Did you kill my husband?"

She shakes her head.

"Skinner?"

She winks. "Can you believe Nicole kept that a secret the whole time? She never told me, even when I asked. It was only on Thursday that she finally opened up. She saw Seymour on the roof. I couldn't let her tell anyone else." She looks at her watch. "Speaking of Nicole, Sesee is going to be over soon. Do you want some more water?"

I nod, and she pours more into my mouth.

"The police are going to find you. They're going to stop you," I say.

She smirks. "Like you did? Do you really think I didn't know you were coming? That I don't have cameras set up? I unlocked the door. I wanted you to come in." She smiles at the surprise in my eyes. "By the way, how's your side? That fall from the fence looked like it hurt."

Mindy replaces the tape and covers my mouth. When she knows it's secure, she stands and bends over and smacks my cheek. "Be good. And don't worry. I'll always take care of Nicole. I'll never let anything happen to her."

She shuts off the light and closes the door, leaving me helplessly staring at the gap of light beneath it.

Chapter 45
Hank

As I turn onto the street I know so well, my phone rings through the speakers in the dashboard, and the caller's name comes up on the screen.

"Whatcha got, Sarah?"

"Hank, I called Kayla Anderson's mother like you asked. She gave you permission to talk to her daughter. I just texted Kayla's number to you. She's expecting your call."

"Wonderful. Great job. Thank you."

She hangs up, and I look over at Carol and raise my eyebrows. I park along the street and click the number in the text. After several seconds, a young female voice answers the phone.

"Hi, is this Kayla Anderson?"

"Yes," she says after a brief stumble. I can tell she has me on speakerphone. Her mother's probably beside her.

"Kayla, my name is Detective Hank Gardner. I'm investigating the disappearance of your schoolmate Nicole Morgan. I understand you're friends with Mindy Decker. Is that right?"

"Yes."

"When was the last time you saw Mindy?"

A pause and a whisper on the other end of the line. "I saw her at school on Thursday."

"Thursday? Did you see her outside of school at all? Or just in school?"

"Just in school."

"Her mother said she was staying at your house this weekend. Are you saying she hasn't been there? You haven't seen her at all?"

"Detective Gardner," an unfamiliar female voice says. This one is more confident and mature. "This is April Anderson, Kayla's mother. I can confirm Kayla hasn't seen Mindy. She hasn't been here."

"Understood, Mrs. Anderson. If either you or Kayla hear from Mindy, will you call me immediately? Do you have my number?"

"We can take it off the caller ID."

"Very good."

We hang up, and I reach for the door handle.

"What are we doing here?" Carol asks.

"Recruiting reinforcements."

We approach the house. After several seconds, the door opens.

Joyce stands in the doorway holding her little dog. "I'm retired," she says.

"No, you're not," I say back. "You're suspended. You still have three months left. Plus, I need your help."

Joyce looks from me to Carol, then waves us inside. We sit in the front room as she rests on the piano bench holding her dog.

"Hank, I can't help you. I'm suspended. If Rigby finds out..."

"Joyce, Skinner was having an affair with one of the students, Mindy Decker. We just arrested him, and it won't be long before the media reports it. Mindy has Nicole. When she knows about Skinner, she's going to run. We've got to find her before that happens."

"Oh no," Joyce says. "Do you know where she might be?"

I shake my head but hold up my phone. "I've got ten places. I figure if Mindy stole Ed's sword, she knows a lot more about him. Sherry Morgan thought the same thing, and now she's missing."

"What?"

I quickly tell Joyce what I found in Ed's house and the fact that Sherry is no longer answering her phone. "She found her, Joyce. And I'm betting she won't keep her alive long. She might already be dead."

"Show me the addresses."

I pull up the note on my phone and hand it to her. She studies it while still holding her dog in the other arm.

"You should have gone to Rigby with this. Not me."

"Rigby isn't my mentor."

We look at each other, then she scans the list again.

"This top one is where we met Ed the other day. I think we can rule it out. It was still being worked on." She moves her finger to the next. "The date on this one shows it's likely still under construction. She wouldn't risk Ed showing up in the house." She slides her finger down to the next. "This one is in Pocatello. No way she went that far." She pulls out her phone and does a quick search of the remaining seven properties. "Four are already up for sale. I doubt she'd go to one of those. She could have a surprise inspection anytime."

"Three options," I say.

Joyce nods. "Three options."

"Three of us."

Joyce shrugs. "Okay. But why not just send cops to each of those houses? You don't need me."

"Oh, believe me, we'll have several cops as backup. But I need people I can trust on-site, controlling the situation. We've likely got a hostage situation, and there's nobody I'd trust more than you. Plus, if Mindy planned all this, she's likely got a surprise or two up her sleeve. I figure we split up and each go to a house with a patrol car."

"Rigby won't like this."

"I don't care. We don't have much time. If Sherry's alive, she won't be for long. If Mindy's leaving, she's not going to take Sherry with her."

Joyce shrugs. "Okay, cowboy, it's your rodeo. Just tell me where I'm going."

I pick an address for each of us, then Carol looks at me.

"I don't have a car."

That's true. I didn't think of that.

"You don't need one," Joyce says and walks away, putting her dog behind a pet fence in the kitchen.

"What do you mean?" Carol asks.

Joyce leads us through the house to the garage. Inside it, there's Joyce's 1977 Ford Bronco and a Toyota Corolla I don't recognize.

"Where's Sam's car?" I ask.

"He's gone this weekend for work. I was bored, so I did some repair work."

"Is that Sherry's car?" I ask.

"Yep."

"You fixed it?"

Joyce winks. "Do you know how boring it is not to have a job? I had to find something to do. Plus, I figured she had enough going on to worry about this." She turns to Carol. "You can drive the Corolla. It doesn't fit me. I'll stick with my Bronco." She turns back to me. "Don't include any backup for the address you give me. If I see anything, I'll call you. I don't want you getting in trouble with Rigby."

Chapter 46

Sherry

Now I'm regretting my choice to ask Mindy for water. It's been several hours, and I don't think I can hold it any longer. I've got to go, and I don't want to do it where I'm sitting. When the light was on earlier, I saw there was a drain in the floor beside the water heater on the opposite wall.

Several minutes ago, Mindy and Nicole returned to the basement, and I can hear them on the other side of the door. Mindy is feeding her.

"Where are we going to go?" Nicole asks.

"I'm not sure yet," Mindy says. "Where would you like to go?"

Nicole thinks for several seconds. "Disneyland."

Mindy laughs as I push against the wall, rising to my feet.

"You like Disneyland? Have you been before?"

"Yep. I love Minnie Mouse. Can we go see her house? Maybe we can sleep there. She likes me. She's my friend."

"Good idea. Maybe so."

I'm on my feet now, and the tape on my ankles is so tight I have to take tiny steps; otherwise, I'll lose my balance.

"Nicole, I need to run out for a minute. When I get back, we're going to leave, okay? I need to get us a bigger, better car to drive."

"Okay."

"Do you want to listen to the Oakridge Boys? I can put a CD on for you. I'll be back before the CD is over."

"Can I color?" Nicole asks.

"Sure. Come over here to the table."

I'm on the other side of the small storage room now. I'm against one wall, pushing my body to feel the water heater. My hand brushes against a pipe, and I jerk in pain. I almost fall but force myself back toward the wall. I close my eyes, breathing through the pain from the burn on my hand. I hear Mindy walk across the room, then the outside door opens and closes.

I try to scream, but nothing comes out. The tape on my mouth is too tight. Plus, Nicole is wearing headphones. Mindy did that on purpose so she won't hear me. Maybe I can get to the door. Maybe I can knock with my knuckles and she'll hear that. I move forward, shuffling about two feet before I trip and fall. I can't stop myself, and I fall face-first on the concrete floor, smashing my head. I want to scream in agony but struggle to get enough air with my nose pressed to the floor. I can taste blood and know I've broken at least one tooth. Worse, I can't hold it any longer, and urine flows out of me.

I cry with my face smashed against the concrete. When I'm done, I scream against the tape and roll onto my back. I look up at the dark ceiling and hear a click in the lock of my door. Oh no! Mindy came back while I was screaming! She's here to kill me. I swallow, preparing myself, thinking about what to do.

The door opens. The light goes on.

"Mama?"

Nicole is standing in the doorway.

Tears spring to my eyes as I look at my beautiful daughter.

She comes over, kneels beside me, and kisses my cheek.

"Mama, you're bleeding," she says, then looks at the tape on my hands and ankles. She rises and leaves the room, only to return a minute later with a knife. She's beside me, pressing the tip of the knife to the tape around my ankles. I've never let her use a knife. How does she know how to do this? Soon, I feel a release, and my legs are free.

She moves up my body to my hands, repeating the same steps. Again, the restraint releases. She giggles as I raise my hand to my face and pull hard on the tape. I cry out and then turn to her. "Oh, my sweet daughter," I say, wrapping my arms around her. "How did you know I was here?"

"You came last night. I kept the secret until Mindy was gone."

I cup her cheek. "You are so smart. I love you so much."

She smiles. "I love you, Mama."

She steps back, and I stand, feeling every bone in my body. My leggings are soaked in urine, but there's no time to deal with that now. I grab Nicole's hand. "Come on, we've got to get out of here."

We walk to the outside door, and I put my ear to it, listening for any sign of Mindy. I put my hand on the door handle, but Nicole reaches out and stops me. "Mama, we can see out the window upstairs."

I pause and look at her. She's right. If we can see out, we can see if Mindy has returned. If I open this door, she could be on the other side. Plus, Mindy says she has cameras on the side of the house. She saw me fall.

Nicole tugs on my hand, and I follow her to the stairs. We go up, and I see all the window blinds are drawn. I go to one and pull up a slat, peering out. It's dark, and I can't see much other than the streetlight across the road. When I look to my right, I hear something downstairs. Mindy has returned. There's a beep when the door opens.

I grip Nicole's hand, and we move to the front door. I can hear Mindy coming up the stairs. I throw the door open and step out, pulling it shut behind me.

"Run," I scream to Nicole as I hold the door shut.

"Mama?"

"Run, my baby. Run!"

Nicole grips the railing and starts down the stairs when I feel the door tug against me. I pull with everything I have, but Mindy is younger and stronger. The door opens, and she comes out. I slap her face as she approaches. It knocks her sideways, then she comes forward, gripping me by the hair. She yanks my head, and I fall, crashing down the stairs.

Nicole is at the bottom of the stairs, looking back as we fight. I try to tell her to run, but the air has been knocked out of my lungs, and I think I have a broken arm. It's scorching with pain. Mindy descends the stairs, and I reach out with my good arm, trying to stop her. She easily steps past me and kicks me in the ribs. I curl up in pain, fighting for air.

Mindy grabs Nicole's hand and drags her to a waiting car. Nicole pulls her hand free and runs to me as Mindy turns back.

"Get your hands off her," I hear a woman's shout and look out toward the street in the direction of the voice. Detective Joyce Powers stands beside the driveway with a gun pointed at Mindy's head. Mindy holds up her hands. "Get on your knees," Joyce says, walking toward her.

Mindy fakes kneeling and takes off running, ducking beneath the car parked in the driveway. Joyce curses and takes off after her as Nicole bends down and cradles my head.

"It's okay, Mama. I'll take care of you."

Chapter 47

Sherry

For the second time in less than a week, I'm waking up in the hospital. But this time, my daughter is beside me. She's seated on a couch on the left side of my bed, watching *Sesame Street*. Oscar the Grouch is talking to Elmo, and he says something that makes her giggle. I can't describe the joy that runs through my body at that sound. Oh, how I've missed it. I look at my body lying in bed and see that my right arm has a brace on it. I feel like I've been hit by a truck. I took a beating in that house with Mindy. It won't be a speedy recovery.

I turn my head to the side and smile at Nicole. "Hey, you."

She looks at me, then gets up and comes to the bed. "Mama, you're awake."

"I am."

"How are you?"

I reach out and put my good hand on her cheek. "I'm a little sore but very happy."

She smiles, and I hear the door to the room open. A doctor and a nurse enter the room.

"Good to see you're awake," the doctor says. He's the same doctor who treated me earlier this week in the ER. "How are you feeling?" he asks as he approaches the bed.

"Sore."

The nurse comes over to stand beside Nicole.

"That would make sense," the doctor says. He shines a light in my eyes and watches me. "Well, the good news is your concussion appears to be gone. You do have a couple of broken ribs, a chipped tooth, and a broken wrist."

"Oh, is that all?" I ask and try to laugh but gasp in pain. I look over at Nicole. She's retreated to the couch, and her eyes are back on the TV.

"We'll keep the brace on your wrist for another couple of days, then have you back for a cast once the swelling has gone down." He looks down at the rest of my body. "Anything else bothering you?"

I shrug. "Hard to tell. I feel pain everywhere."

He looks at me closely. "Any area worse than any other?"

I shake my head.

There's a knock on the door, and a man pokes his head around the corner.

"Can I help you?" the nurse says, taking a couple steps toward him.

"Just coming to check on her," Detective Gardner says. "I can come back later."

"Good timing," the doctor says. "We were just finishing up. Come on in."

Detective Gardner enters the room, followed by Officer Levy. They stand to the side while the nurse refills my water and the doctor asks a couple more questions. When they're done, the doctor and nurse leave, and the detectives approach the bed.

Detective Gardner looks at Nicole. "How are you doing, Nicole?"

Nicole doesn't take her eyes off the TV screen. "Fine."

Detective Gardner chuckles, then turns to me. "New episode?"

I shrug. "New to me."

He smiles. "Well, how are you feeling?"

"Amazing," I say and look over at Nicole. "Thank you both for your help. I appreciate it more than you could ever know."

"We're just glad it worked out."

"Where's Detective Powers?"

He shrugs. "Home, I think. She's a little sore herself."

"Oh?"

"Yeah, well, as you know, Mindy took off running. Joyce didn't want to shoot her but couldn't let her get away. She chased her for a couple blocks, but Mindy was too fast. Especially after Joyce took a spill on some ice and twisted her ankle."

"Oh no," I say.

"Ah, she'll be all right. But I do have some bad news."

"What?"

He looks down at the bed. "Mindy got away."

"What?"

"It was several minutes before we could get there, and in that time, she disappeared."

"She's still on the loose?"

He nods. "It won't be for long. There aren't many places she could go with a warrant out for her arrest. We'll find her."

Without realizing it, I see Nicole has moved over to stand beside him. She looks like a baby compared to him. She tugs on his sleeve, and he looks down at her.

"I know a secret," she says.

He nods and pulls a paper from his pocket and unfolds it. It's a drawing. I recognize it immediately. It was in Nicole's room. "Is it about this?" he asks.

Nicole looks at him, then turns and looks at me.

"Go ahead, honey, you can tell him."

She looks back up at him. "My principal hurt my daddy."

"Principal Skinner did something to your daddy?"

She nods and points to the picture. "He pushed him off the roof."

"You're sure it was Principal Skinner? It wasn't Mindy?"

She shakes her head. "Mr. Skinner."

He bends down and puts a hand on her shoulder. "Thank you for telling me."

She nods and comes over to the bed. "Mama, can I color?"

"I don't have any colors, sweetie."

"Let me see if I can find you some," Officer Levy says.

"Thank you," Nicole says, and Levy leaves the room.

"Honey," I reach out to hold Nicole's hand, "I'm so proud of you. That was very brave what you did."

Nicole winks and smiles.

"Now I have something I need to tell you."

"Okay, Mama."

I look over at Detective Gardner. He's standing with his arms crossed, staring at the floor.

"Nicky, honey, your grandma was really sick. She had cancer. Do you know about cancer?"

Nicole nods.

"Remember the last day I took you to school? The day Mindy took you?"

She nods.

"Grandma had to go to the hospital. She couldn't get better and, well, she died."

Nicole's blue eyes stare at me, and I'm not sure what she understands.

"So, the cancer finally won, Mama?"

"What do you mean, 'finally won'?"

"Grandma told me about the cancer. She told me that she was fighting with the cancer but the cancer was winning. She said it was okay, because she'd be with Grandpa again when the cancer won."

Tears come to my eyes, and I smile. "That's right, baby. Grandma is with Grandpa again."

Officer Levy comes back with a coloring book and a big box of crayons. She moves the rolling table in front of the couch, and Nicole comes over and sits down.

"We're going to go now," Detective Gardner says and comes forward to grip my good hand. "The doctors say you'll be able to go home tomorrow. We're going to keep a police car in front of your house until Mindy's found."

"Thank you."

Officer Levy shakes my hand, then they turn to leave, but I call them back.

"Yes?" Gardner says.

"Will you tell Detective Powers how much I appreciate her? If she hadn't been there..."

He nods. "I'll tell her."

They leave, and I look over at Nicole. She's coloring furiously, all in one color.

I lower the bed rails and swing my legs off the bed, then shuffle over to her, gasping in pain with every step. I sit beside her, and she just goes on coloring. Black covers the page. I reach out and put my hand on hers, and she stops and looks at me.

"Nikki, it's going to be okay. Grandma's okay. Roy is okay, and so is your daddy."

She looks confused. "I know, Mama."

I take the crayon from her and hold it up. "Then why are you only coloring with this color when there are so many others in the box?"

She looks at the box, then at the picture in the book. "Because that's what people do."

"What do you mean?"

"When someone dies, Mama. People wear black, and everything is black. That's why I'm coloring my pictures black."

Chapter 48
Hank

"Gardner, come with me."

I lean out from my cubicle and see Captain Rigby standing down the hall by the exit to the police headquarters. He's wearing his coat and holding his keys. Levy looks over at me with a questioning look, and I shrug and stand.

"Get your coat," the captain says.

"Do you want Levy also?"

He shakes his head, and I put on my jacket as I walk toward him. He motions with his head for me to follow, and we walk out the front doors. His car is in the front, not parked in the back. He walks to the driver's side, and I get in the passenger seat.

He starts the car, and the radio comes on as he pulls out of the parking lot.

"What kind of music do you like?" he asks.

Why does everyone keep asking me that?

"A little of everything. Mostly rap and R and B," I say.

"Joyce hasn't rubbed off on you yet?"

I look at him and see his slight smile.

"What do you mean?"

He turns the wheel and shrugs. "I just thought by now you'd be a rock fan. I know that's all Joyce will let you listen to."

"Yeah, that's true."

"So, you aren't a fan yet? You aren't listening to AC/DC when nobody's around?"

What is he getting at here? He looks at me and grins and I frown. I look out the window and see we're in Joyce's neighborhood. He makes several turns and pulls into her driveway, shutting off the car.

"Come on," he says and climbs out.

I follow, curious to see what he's up to.

We reach the front door and he knocks. After several seconds, the video doorbell greets us. It's Joyce.

"What do you want?"

"To talk to you," Rigby says, looking at the camera.

"What about?"

"Let us in, and you'll find out."

She's quiet for a moment. "Come in. It's not locked."

We enter and walk down the hall to the back of the house. Joyce is sitting on the couch, her leg propped up with a medical boot on one foot. She's watching a romance movie and has her hand in a bowl of popcorn. Rigby stands in front of the TV, and she leans to the side to see past him.

"Pause the movie for a minute," he says.

She looks up at him. "No. I don't work for you anymore."

"Yes, you do."

"Nope, you suspended me."

"You deserved it."

"So?"

"So, you've been gone long enough. Now I want you back."

She shakes her head and pauses the movie, leaning back in her seat. "I don't want to."

"Why not?"

"I lost the girl. I'm too old for this. Leave me to my romance and popcorn."

He comes around and sits beside her on the couch. I remain standing by the side. "You are old but not *too* old. We need you. Come back."

She shakes her head, and I sigh and roll my eyes. Both of them look over at me.

"When is all this going to stop?" I ask and then look at my watch.

"What?" Joyce asks with popcorn sticking out of her mouth.

"This whole thing." I raise the pitch of my voice. "Oh, I'm being insubordinate when I never have been before." I point at Rigby and drop my voice. "I'm going to suspend you to teach you a lesson." I shake my head. "Just admit you did all this to test me. I'm not buying the suspended bit."

Their mouths drop open, and they look at each other.

"I thought we were pretty good?" Joyce says to him.

"So did I," Rigby responds.

"Well, you weren't," I say and look at Joyce. "So, are you coming back or what? Did I prove myself worthy yet?"

She shrugs, takes another handful of popcorn, and pushes play on the movie. "I could have done with a bit more begging, but if you insist, I'll come back on one condition."

"What?"

"You trust yourself more."

I frown. "I trust myself."

"Do you? Always? Be honest. You compare yourself to me, and you've got to stop that. You and I have different strengths. We might do things differently, but that doesn't mean one way is better than the other. This case proves it. You were fantastic."

Chapter 49

Hank

We walk into the jail and pass through security, greeting the guards. Joyce is out of her boot now, opting for a lace-up brace instead. Her gait is slow, but she's able to put pressure on her ankle. As we walk down the hallway, Officer Levy walks toward us.

"Hi, Carol," Joyce says.

"Good to see you're out of the boot."

"Yeah, I didn't like how it went with my pantsuit."

Carol smiles, then looks up at me and brushes past us down the hall.

I call after her. "Hey, Carol?"

She turns.

"Thanks for helping me out. You were great. I look forward to working with you more."

"Thanks," she says and walks away.

We keep walking.

"Do you think she's mad?" I ask.

"I don't know about mad, but I don't think she's happy to be staying a cop when she thought she was being promoted to detective. Would you be?"

"Do you think she blames me?"

Joyce stops and looks up at me. "Does it matter?"

We stare at each other for several seconds, then she starts walking again. We reach the door to the interrogation room, and Joyce opens it. Principal Skinner is sitting at the table with his attorney beside him. Skinner is wearing the standard-issue prison uniform with shackles on his wrists. His attorney stands and shakes our hands. He's a lean fellow with blond hair. He looks very young.

After we dispense with the pleasantries, Joyce gets down to business, opening the file in front of her.

"Mr. Skinner, we appreciate you taking the time to meet with us today. We understand from your attorney that you're willing to assist us with our investigation in exchange for our recommendation to the district attorney for a more lenient sentence. Is that correct?"

Both Skinner and his attorney nod.

"I want to make it clear that we can only recommend a reduced sentence. We have no control over the actual sentence given."

"But you will recommend it. And both the district attorney and judge consider your recommendations," Skinner's attorney says, more to him than to us.

"I understand," Skinner says.

Joyce nods. "We don't have many questions for you. Most of what we want to know revolves around your relationship with Mindy Decker, a student at the high school where you were the principal."

Joyce takes out a pair of reading glasses and grips a pen. She looks down at her sheet, then back up at Skinner. "How did your relationship with Mindy begin?"

"She was a student at my school."

Joyce shakes her head. "I'm sorry. I should have said, how did your sexual relationship with Mindy begin?"

Skinner glares at her, and his attorney shakes his head. "Detective?"

Joyce looks at him innocently. "Oh, I'm sorry. Was the relationship not sexual? Did they just play patty-cake together?"

The attorney stares at her, then looks over to Skinner and shrugs. "Go ahead."

"She put sexy pictures of herself in the drawers of my desk at school."

"Sexy pictures? Like nudes?"

Skinner's cheeks burn. "Yes."

"I guess you liked them," Joyce says and makes a note on her sheet without looking up. "And when did you and Mindy first start having sex?"

Principal Skinner shakes his head and sighs. "Shortly after."

"When was that?"

"About a year ago this coming January."

"Uh-huh," Joyce says, still looking down. "And you knew she was only seventeen years old?"

He sighs again. "Yes."

"Where would you meet for these rendezvous? I imagine being married and having sex with one of your students, you needed to keep things pretty quiet."

"You don't have to say it like that," Skinner says, his brow furrowed and his voice sharp.

Joyce looks up. "I know. But everything I said was true. No?"

The attorney sits back and folds his arms. Skinner looks at him, then back at Joyce.

"Mostly in cars. Either hers or mine."

"Romantic," Joyce says. "Where were the cars parked?"

"Detective, does that matter?" the attorney says.

"It might," Joyce says. "I don't know yet."

The attorney sighs and motions for Skinner to answer.

"At secluded spots. Mostly parks and places like that."

"Did you ever have sex at school?"

Skinner looks down.

"I'll take that as a yes," Joyce says. "Did anyone ever see you at one of these rendezvous? Perhaps at the park?"

Skinner hesitates.

"Come on, Seymour," Joyce says. "We're working together now."

"Yeah, someone saw us."

"Who?"

"Ron Morgan."

"That's Nicole's father?"

"Yes."

Joyce makes a note on her sheet. "How did you know he saw you?"

Skinner shuffles his feet. "He came to the school the next day and confronted me."

"What did he say?"

"He said he was going to go to the police unless I confessed."

"What did you do?"

"I begged him to give me another day. I asked him to allow me to tell my wife before I went to the police."

"What did he say?"

Skinner looks up from the table. "He said he would give me the weekend."

"Then what happened?"

"That night, I met Mindy and told her. She begged me not to tell my wife. She wanted to run away together. I told her I had to." He stops and rubs his hands together. "The next day, Ron fell from his roof and died shortly after."

"Hmm," Joyce says. "That's a heck of a coincidence, wouldn't you say?"

He doesn't respond, and his attorney frowns and looks at him.

"Were you there when Ron fell? Did you have anything to do with it?"

Skinner shakes his head.

"What about Mindy? Did she cause his fall?"

Skinner shrugs.

"You don't know?"

"Not for sure. I never asked her, and she never told me."

"Hmm," Joyce says and makes a note on her sheet. "Then what happened with Mindy? Did you break it off?"

"For a few weeks."

"That must have been tough," Joyce says, and Skinner glares at her. "So, after a few weeks, you got back to screwing one of your students. I bet you gave up on the parks, huh? Needed somewhere more discreet? Then where did you go?"

Skinner looks down.

"You started sneaking into vacant houses, didn't you?"

Skinner looks up with surprise, then nods.

"Houses under construction?"

He nods again.

"How did you learn of the houses?"

"I didn't know. Mindy knew about them."

Joyce leans forward. "How did she know?"

"She never told me."

"You never asked?"

He looks up. "I did once, but she told me not to worry about it."

Joyce takes off her glasses and looks at him. "Did you know Mindy was holding Nicole Morgan captive? Did you know it was in one of those houses?"

Skinner shakes his head.

"See," Joyce says, pointing at him. "That's where I just don't think we can believe you. I think you knew and chose not to tell us."

Skinner shakes his head. "I didn't know. I swear."

"You're a liar," Joyce snarls.

"Detective," his attorney says, holding up a hand.

Joyce flips to another page in the file. "I have a sworn statement from a witness who saw Seymour Skinner on the roof of Ron Morgan's home the day he fell. I have another statement from another witness who swears Mindy Decker told her that Seymour Skinner pushed Ron Morgan to his death." Joyce leans forward. "You've got one last shot, Seymour. Tell us where Mindy Decker is, or we're adding a first-degree murder charge to your rap sheet."

Skinner and his attorney stare at each other.

"You'd better tell them," the attorney says.

Skinner bites his cheek. "My wife's family has a house on the Utah side of Bear Lake. She might be there."

Chapter 50

Sherry

My door opens, and I turn over in bed. Nicole stands in my doorway, looking frightened. I sit up. "What is it, honey?"

"Mama? There's a sound coming from downstairs."

"What kind of sound?" I swing my legs out of bed and wrap my robe around me.

"A scratching sound," she says as I come close.

"Stay here," I say and go past her down the hall. I stop at the top of the stairs. Mindy is still out there. They haven't found her yet. I go to the front door and look out the window. The police car is still parked outside. I relax and go back up the stairs and check the clock in the kitchen. It's almost eight. We slept longer than I thought we would.

"Nikki, honey," I say, calling her.

She tentatively pokes her head out of my room.

"Come here, honey. It's okay."

She's hesitant but finally walks down the hall after more prodding.

I hug her and then cup her face in my good hand. "Do you know what day it is?"

She looks past me at the tree in our living room. "Christmas?"

I wink. "Yup. Do you want to see what Santa brought?"

She giggles, and we walk into the living room. Her eyes go wide as she looks at the presents under the tree. There are several coloring books, a new Oakridge Boys poster, a new red backpack, and several outfits.

"Open your stocking," I tell her, pointing to the fireplace mantel.

She goes over and pulls down her stocking, looking through it. A yelp sounds from downstairs, and she hears it. "Mama," she says and comes over to me.

I hug her to me, feeling her body shake. "It's okay, Nikki." I pull back and look into her eyes. "You have one more present. But it's downstairs. Do you want me to go with you to get it?"

She nods, and I take her by the hand and lead her downstairs. We go down the hall to my mother's room, and Domo can hear us coming. He barks, and Nicole pushes into me.

"It's okay, honey."

I open the door, and Domo comes bounding out. He sees Nicole and jumps up on her, licking her hand. Her mouth drops open in shock.

"This is your new dog," I tell her.

She looks up at me and giggles, then bends down and pets his head.

"I think he needs to go outside to do his business. Can you let him out the back door?"

Nicole nods and walks with him up the stairs as I follow. She opens the back door, and Domo goes out as I sit down at the kitchen table. She remains at the door, watching him. After a few minutes, he comes back, and she lets him in. She kneels, and he licks her face.

"Do you want to feed him?" I ask.

She nods, and I get out his food and bowls. I help her as she fills both his water and food bowls. He eats as she pets him.

"What do you want to call him?" I ask.

She looks back at me. "Sammy."

"Sammy? Why Sammy?"

She shrugs. "I like that name."

"Sammy it is. Should I make some breakfast?"

She nods.

"What would you like?"

"Maybe French toast?"

I nod. "Sounds great. Do you want to get your new coloring books? You can color at the table while I make it."

"Okay."

I get out the eggs, bread, butter, and milk while she sets her things on the kitchen table. Once I get the French toast cooking, I go over and sit down beside her. She's got a coloring book with puppies, and she's coloring one page.

"That's a pretty picture. Is that dog Sammy?"

She nods.

"I like all the colors on the page."

She stops and looks up at me. "Thank you for the doggy, Mama. I love him."

Chapter 51

Hank

I get out of the car and approach the Rich County SWAT vehicle parked on the side of the road. Joyce and I arrived five minutes ago from Idaho Falls. Since learning of this house from Skinner, we've been in contact with Rich County, Utah, law enforcement. They've been surveying the house and confirmed a positive sighting less than an hour ago. The burly officer rolls down his window as I draw near.

"Detective Hank Gardner," I say, extending my hand. He takes it through the open window. "Which house is she in?"

He points to the roofline of a house a block away.

"You're sure it's her?"

He nods. "She got a haircut and dyed it platinum, but it's her."

I nod. "What's the plan?"

"We've got plenty of officers here. It should be pretty simple. She's alone."

"She might have a weapon."

He nods. "Understood. We'll be cautious."

"Where would you like us?"

"Doesn't matter. Stay in your vehicle. I'll let you know when it's safe to come in."

"You got it," I say and shake his hand again.

I get back in the car, and we follow the SWAT vehicle as it approaches the house. I park along the side of the road and wait as officers pour out of the vehicle and surround the house. The leader gets out a bullhorn and speaks to Mindy. After a few seconds, the drapes in the house part, and she looks out and then closes them.

"Mindy," he says. "You've got nowhere to go. Come out. I'll give you two minutes before we come in. The clock is running."

A minute passes without any movement, then the front door opens, and Mindy stands on the porch.

"My name is Ginger. I don't know Mindy. Who are you? Why are you here?"

The SWAT officers point their guns toward her and take several steps closer.

"Come away from the house, and we can talk about it."

Mindy looks beyond the officers to me as I stand beside our car. Joyce remains in the passenger seat. I can see she recognizes me, and I certainly know her. We stare at each other for several seconds, then she whips around and reenters the house.

After another minute, the SWAT leader calls out to her again, telling her to come out or they'll be forced to enter. She doesn't respond, and he gives instructions to his officers when an explosion rocks the house, and flames erupt from within. Officers breach the front door and enter the home. After less than a minute, the leader comes out and approaches our vehicle.

"She blew herself up," he says. "She used the gas stove to fill the air with propane. She lit a match and..." He makes an explosive gesture with his hands.

"She's dead?" I ask.

He nods as the fire department arrives. In less than five minutes, the flames are out, and the house is cleared. Joyce and I enter and confirm it's Mindy. We talk logistics with the officer and then head out the door.

Ten minutes later, we're back on the road, headed home. As we pass the lake, I look at Joyce. "Why do you think she did it?"

Joyce looks at me, raises an eyebrow, then looks out over the lake. "She was young and probably decided she had nothing left to live for. She couldn't face the prospect of coming back home with everyone knowing who she was and what she did. She lost hope."

"What do you believe about their relationship?"

"What do you mean?"

"Do you think she really did seduce him?"

She shrugs. "Based on what they told others, it sounds like it." She turns away from the window and looks at me. "Speaking of losing hope..."

I frown.

"How many Cokes do I owe you about now?"

I chuckle. "I think I lost count."

She smiles. "Yeah, while I was on the couch eating popcorn and crying to romance movies, I was thinking. I think that game is played. Even if you won't admit it, I know you love eighties and nineties rock now."

"I won't confirm or deny."

She smiles.

"So, what are you proposing?"

"Oh no. You've proven you can be the senior detective now. That was my game. Now it's your turn to choose."

I grin and look back at the road. "So, you want to listen to *my* music now?"

"I didn't say that."

"You didn't not say it." My phone, as usual, is connected to the car's Bluetooth. I bring up Spotify and hold the phone so she can't see what I'm doing. "I'll tell you what, if you can name this song, I'll forgive the debt of all the Cokes."

She smiles. "Every last one?"

I nod.

"Deal."

I hold up a finger. "But if you don't get it, I control the radio for the remainder of our partnership."

She eyes me warily. "No gangster rap."

I shake my head. "You can't make conditions."

She sighs. "Fine."

I nod and hit play on my phone.

California love, we-ooh

California knows how to party

California knows how to party

In the city of LA

In the city of good ol' Watts

In the city, city of Compton

We keep it rockin', we keep it rockin' (Ooh)

She looks over at me. "Is this music?"

I chuckle. "This is one of my favorite songs. I admit, I do like your rock, but nothing compares to this."

She shakes her head. "You're insane."

"Fair enough. But that's not the name of the song."

She bites her cheek and stares at the dashboard. "Is it called 'California Love'?"

I nod. "I'm impressed. But that's only half of it."

I took it easy on her for the song. She'll never get the name of the artist.

"This is old," she says.

I shrug. "That's why I thought it would be fair for you."

She glares at me. "Not cool."

"Who sings it?"

She raises her fingers to her lips and drums them. "Hmm." After a few seconds, she turns to me and winks. "He was shot in Vegas. Cold case. Never solved."

I frown, feeling my heart drop. "What's his name?"

"2Pac," she says and sticks her tongue out at me.

I shake my head, floored that she knew that. "Not just him."

She shakes her head. "He's the one known for this song."

I shrug. "Yeah, but he isn't the only artist credited for it."

She winks again. "It's 2Pac's song, even if Dr. Dre collaborated with him on it."

My mouth drops open, and I stare at her.

"Never try and beat the master at her own game."

Chapter 52

Sherry

I pull the car into the parking lot and find a parking space near the front of the building. When I shut off the car, I turn and look at Nicole. She's seated in the back seat, her new backpack in her lap. "Are you ready?"

She nods and unhooks her seat belt. I get out of the car and meet her on the passenger side. She takes my hand, and we walk into the high school. There are kids all around. Today is the first day back after the holidays. It's January second, and there's a whole new feel to the school. It feels fresh and new. Kids see us coming and wave, greeting Nicole. She smiles and giggles as she acknowledges all of them. Once inside, we walk down the hall. There's a group of cowboys standing around a row of lockers. They turn and see us, and one boy approaches.

"Hey, Nicole," he says, turning to the side. "Wanna smack it?" He smiles and sticks his butt out toward her. He's wearing tight jeans with a large belt buckle. Before I can stop her, she giggles and spanks him. He jumps and rubs it, pretending to be in pain.

"There you go, apple head," she says.

I shake my head and pull her forward.

When we reach the classroom, I stop at the door, not wanting to enter. Nicole tugs on my hand, then looks up at me. I wink at her. "You don't need me to go in there. You go ahead."

"Okay, Mama. See you after school?"

"You betcha."

She hugs me, then goes in. I stand back so I can still see into the classroom, but they can't see me. Georgette Thomas is in the front of the room. Ty and Marilyn are already seated at their desks.

"Welcome back, Nicole," Ms. Thomas says. "Go ahead and hang up your coat and backpack, then come sit down."

Ty and Marilyn turn in their chairs so they can see her. "Welcome back, Nicole," they shout in unison.

Nicole hangs up her coat, then her backpack, and finds her seat. Ty aims the camera on his iPad at her and tells her, "Say cheese." My eyes become cloudy as I watch her smile for the camera. She sits down, and a large boy brushes past me, almost bowling me over. I look up to see that Shawn is entering the room. He didn't even feel his collision with me. When he enters, he stops and stands at the back, looking at everyone.

"Welcome back, Shawn," Ms. Thomas says. "Hang up your coat and come sit down."

Shawn heads over to the coatrack as all three kids turn to look at him.

"Yeah," Ty says when he sees him and pretends to play the drums as Nicole and Marilyn wave to Shawn. When Shawn sits down, Ty tells him to smile and takes his picture.

"Okay," Ms. Thomas says. "Now that everyone's back, we have some work to do. We're going to do some reading. I want you all to get out your workbooks."

I look over at the one empty desk. It's still full of balloons and cards. Although there's been a great amount of healing, the classroom will never be complete again.

I stay for five more minutes, then back away and walk out of the school. When I reach my car, I brush my hand over the front fender. My right hand is still in a cast; it will be for another few weeks, but it's not hurting as much as it did. I still can't believe that it was Detective Powers who fixed my car. What can't that woman do? She delivered it to me after I got out of the hospital. I just thought she had picked it up until Detective Gardner told me she was the one who had fixed it.

I unlock the door with my left hand and get behind the wheel. I push the button to start it, then sit, staring at the school. So much has changed in the last two weeks. So much has changed in me. I'm still processing the knowledge that Seymour Skinner, my husband's childhood friend, was the one who killed him. Pushed him from our roof, and Nicole saw it! For half a year, she held that secret, shielding me from the information. I realize now that she was protecting me. She didn't want me to know because she didn't want to hurt me. And all that time, I thought I was shielding her. I never allowed her to be free. I should have spent my time freeing Nicole.

I put the car in drive and pull out of the parking lot. I don't want to go home, at least not yet. Instead, I drive to the cemetery. I enter and drive up the third row and stop in front of two headstones. One says Ron Morgan, devoted father and husband. The one beside it bears the name of Don and Beverly Fullmer. All three of them lie here, side by side. Someday, Nicole and I will join them. But I'm so grateful it's not now. We still have so much left to do.

I blow a kiss to the stones, then drive away. I turn on the radio and hear a song I haven't heard in years. It's a rock song, and I don't even remember who sings it. But there's a line that hits me harder than ever before. I'm listening to the song with a new perspective.

Since you've gone I've been lost without a trace

I dream at night, I can only see your face

I look around, but it's you I can't replace

I feel so cold, and I long for your embrace

That's exactly how I felt when Nicole was gone. I lost her for only two days, but never have I felt more alone. The winter felt like it would never end. The snow fell endlessly.

But now, the sunshine streams through my car window. I'm no longer cold. I'm no longer afraid. As I turn the wheel of the car with one hand, I know life isn't going to be easy. But I also know that Nicole is going to help me through it.

Afterword
The Real Nicole

Nicole wearing her Oakridge Boys sweatshirt

My sister, Nicole Maughan, was born on July 11, 1975. My parents, worrying they couldn't have children, adopted my older brother less than a year before. Suddenly, they went from no kids to two under a year old.

Nicole was a beautiful, healthy, happy baby. One morning, when she was nine months old, my mother noticed she wasn't awake at her usual time. When she entered her bedroom to wake her, she found vomit on the mattress of the crib. She picked up Nicole and couldn't rouse her, then ran and called for an ambulance.

Nicole was rushed to Primary Children's Hospital, where several tests were conducted. One scan showed a massive tumor near her brain. Doctors and nurses operated, and thankfully, Nicole survived. Less than two years later, my parents noticed something wasn't right and took her back in. Scans confirmed she had two more tumors. Again, Nicole underwent multiple surgeries to remove the tumors. They also used radiation to prevent the tumors from returning. Mom says they no longer do that to children because of the complications it can cause.

Nicole was never supposed to live beyond nine months old. Time and time again, she proved the doctors wrong. I was born less than four years after her and grew up alongside her. Although *Freeing Nicole* is a fictional story, the character of Nicole is based on her. She absolutely loved the Oakridge Boys, *Sesame Street*, and *The Princess Bride*. She loved to color, adored the color red, and was the kindest, sweetest person you could ever meet.

She would ride her bicycle around the neighborhood and stop and talk to neighbors and friends. We had a beagle named Sammy. At the high school she attended, she actually did smack the butts of several of the boys who belonged to a group called Cowboy Corner.

Nicole was incredibly kind. If you made her mad, the only insults she would ever fling at you were "apple head' or "bright eyes." Georgette was a real teacher. The only one I can ever remember Nicole not liking. She would tell her not to eat any french fries. Shawn Luelan was a real boy at her school and her boyfriend.

When I was a senior in high school, Nicole got up one night and went to the bathroom. She had a seizure. Seizures were a common occurrence in our house. Nicole would have them almost every day. Once she had one in the grocery store, and they brought the fire truck. After sleeping for several minutes, she'd wake and have no memory of what had just happened. But on that day, she fell and would never recover. The fall caused a subdermal hematoma in her skull. My entire senior year of high school, Nicole was in the hospital. As a family, we ate almost every dinner at the hospital, wondering if she would make it. It was an extremely difficult time for our family, especially my parents.

During the surgery to fix the hematoma, she contracted an infection in her skull. Complications ensued. This resulted in the removal of part of her skull. For the last two years of her life, she remained bedridden, never able to perform even the simplest of functions. My mother cared for her daily, feeding her through a tube and changing her bedding and diapers. She did everything for her.

On April 20, 1999, weighing almost nothing, Nicole's spirit finally left her body. She was a tiny person, barely four feet tall, but had a spirit larger than Fezzik, the giant in *The Princess Bride*. Nicole could reach people many found unreachable. I once saw her make a crotchety old man, who nobody thought could smile, laugh hysterically. He would seek her out whenever he saw her.

Nicole was truly a blessing in my life, and I count myself lucky to be her brother. Thank you for reading my story and for journeying with me down memory lane, remembering how much I love and miss my little big sister.

D.J. Maughan

Epilogue

Follow the link below or scan the QR code for a free short story about Hank and Joyce's first day working together.

Trick or Death

A Halloween story

A widower calls the police on Halloween claiming someone has vandalized his home. When the detectives arrive, they learn the police had questioned him in the past. Does he have something to hide? Brent Spencer has been alone for years. After his wife unexpectedly died, he has been occupying his time by keeping his home in pristine condition. Now, he's furious when he finds someone has vandalized it.

As detectives, Gardner and Powers arrive at the residence on their first day working together, they quickly realize Mr. Spencer isn't telling them the entire story.

Why does Mr. Spencer want them there? What is he planning?

https://dl.bookfunnel.com/53h51ox0pp

Also by D.J. Maughan

D.J. Maughan novels by date of publication

Vanished From Budapest – published December 9, 2022. Peter Andrassy novel one. Psychological thriller. Standalone.

The Villains Mask – published March 15, 2023. Prequel to Vanished from Budapest. Short story. Standalone.

Pursuit of Demons – published March 17, 2023. Peter Andrassy novel two. Book one of the Vanished series.

Revealing the Shadows – published July 23, 2023. Peter Andrassy novel three. Book two of the Vanished series.

Chasing the Wicked – published November 22, 2023. Peter Andrassy novel four. Book three of the Vanished series.

One Desperate Life – published April 26, 2024. Standalone gripping thriller.

Idaho Fall – published October 1, 2024. Hank and Joyce novel one. Standalone twisty whodunit.

The First Five Peter Andrassy Thrillers box set – published October 12, 2024. Available in eBook only through Amazon.

9-1-1 – published March 27, 2025. Peter Andrassy novel five. Crime thriller. Standalone.

Trick or Death – published October 1, 2025. Hank and Joyce short story. Standalone.

Freeing Nicole – published October 1, 2025. Hank and Joyce novel two. Standalone twisty whodunit.

About the author

*Superman D.J. with
Nicole supervising*

D.J. Maughan is an avid reader, event manager, father, husband, public speaker, and award-winning author. No surprise that he writes in the Thriller/Mystery genre, that's what he loves to read. He craves the unexpected and strives to provide that to his readers. He seeks inspiration everywhere, especially while studying and visiting diverse places and cultures. Whether jumping from a cliff in Hawaii or hiking the Plitvica Lakes in Croatia, he's in heaven as long as his wife and four sons are at his side.

Acknowledgements

Thank you to my beta readers. Your insights helped shape this novel. Brooke Maughan, Lupe Merino, Laurie Clark, Luke Barber, Jerry Paskett, Paul Gyorke, Laura Martin, Debbie Altom, Heather Brandt, Katie Jablonka, Heather Kerber, Jennifer Harper, Hannah Exey, Angie Kellett, Jessica Evans, Erin Sterett, Dawn Resue, Rachel Browning, Jessica Earles, Samantha Becker, Michelle Van Hemelryck, Kelsey Housman, Reanne TDHD, and Michelle Ramsey. A big thank you to my editor, Jonathan Starke. I also want to thank Amanda Cox, my cover designer. I appreciate your help and kindness.